UNCHIPPED: LAURA

THE UNCHIPPED SERIES
THE MEETING: AN UNCHIPPED SHORT STORY
UNCHIPPED: KAARINA
UNCHIPPED: WILLIAM
UNCHIPPED: ENYD
UNCHIPPED: LUNA
UNCHIPPED: THE RESORT
CHIPPED: LAURA
CHIPPED: DENNIS
CHIPPED: MARGARET
CHIPPED: JOVAN
CHIPPED: THE REVENANT
DECHIPPED: KRISTIAN
DECHIPPED: MARIA
DECHIPPED: OWENA
DECHIPPED: IRIS
DECHIPPED: THE DOWNLOAD
RECHIPPED: CITY OF SERBIA
RECHIPPED: CITY OF ENGLAND
RECHIPPED: CITY OF CALIFORNIA
RECHIPPED: CITY OF FINLAND
RECHIPPED: THE BUTTON

COMING SOON!
THE MACHINA DEUS SERIES (2024)
SERF GIRL
FAMA GIRL
SLUM GIRL

UNCHIPPED: LAURA

TAYA DEVERE

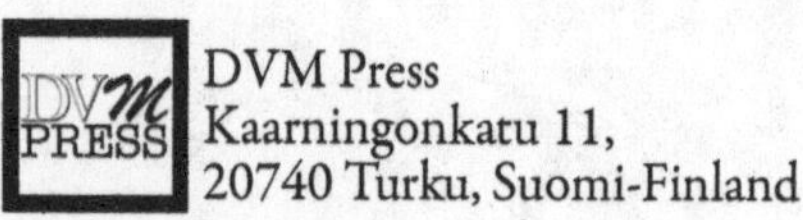

DVM Press
Kaarningonkatu 11,
20740 Turku, Suomi-Finland

www.dvmpress.com
www.tayadevere.com

This is a work of fiction. Names, characters, places, and incidents either are the products of the author's imagination or are used fictitiously. Any resemblance to actual persons, living or dead, businesses, companies, events, or locales is entirely coincidental.

For information about special discounts available for bulk purchases, sales promotions, fund-raising and educational needs, contact sales@dvmpress.com

ISBN 978-952-7404-17-1 First Ebook Edition
ISBN 978-952-7404-18-8 First Print Edition

Cover Design © 2020 by Deranged Doctor Design - www.derangeddoctordesign.com

Cover Spine Design © 2022 by Chris DeVere

Editing by Christopher Scott Thompson, Lindsay Fara Kaplan, and Elle Fort

To those who have made mistakes in life.
To those wrestling with regret, shame, or sorrow.
You are not your past. You are what you do today.

CONTENTS

KNOCK, KNOCK

A short story in the world of the Unchipped series

The Resort, Iceland 2089

Her eyes. Their eerie, neon-blue glow. That's what first told Sanna something odd was happening. The lady had turned into a robot in front of her. First, her eyes started to shine, and she stopped talking. Then, her head started to twitch and tic. She stood by the front door, holding a rifle, gazing into the wooden boards as though she could see right through them. Once the glimmer in her eyes started to dim and finally faded away, her legs and arms turned into noodles. Now she lies there, eyes glazed over like a porcelain doll. Her pale, limp hand is close enough for Sanna to touch.

Is she dead? Or just resting? Should Sanna shake the lifeless Niina awake, or would touching the lady give her some sort of a robot virus?

Mirroring each other's movements, Sanna and Owena get up from the floor. Sanna backs away from the woman and whispers Owena's name.

Because she's the older of the two, Sanna feels as if she should protect the five-year-old Owena, but instead of following Sanna, the little girl walks over to the dead robot lady and kicks her lifeless foot. The sneaker moves briefly from side to side.

"Owena, stop."

The little girl turns to look at Sanna. "What for?"

"Because."

Owena kicks the other foot. Sanna holds her breath, stands, and stares, not sure what to do next. How did all this happen? Why had Niina—the robot thing stretched out on the floor—suddenly locked them inside the cottage, refusing to let them leave? It's been days since Markus last came knocking, or Micky or Ava or anyone else. Why had they stopped? And why had Niina refused to let them in?

But adults are stupid like that. Unpredictable. It's a rare treat if they explain themselves. Usually, they just give one answer to any and, what it sometimes seems, *all* questions; "Because I said so." That's why Sanna hadn't asked Niina anything. Not even before her eyes turned piercing blue.

Why can't we go play with the dogs?

Can we still go to the poolside tonight for story time?

Why can't Owena play with the axe?

Why does my head hurt and why do my ears ring?

What's that glow in your eyes?

Owena kneels next to Niina's body. The rifle is stuck underneath the woman's arm. Owena grabs the handle and tugs until the weapon is released from its trap. The barrel trailing against the floorboards, Owena walks away from Niina, dragging the gun. Then she hands it to Sanna.

"Why me?" Sanna asks.

"I'm too small."

"But I don't know how to shoot." When Owena doesn't answer, Sanna continues. "And who are we shooting? Who's out there?"

"Satan," Owena says without a blink. Then she walks straight to the front door. "And you don't have to shoot with it."

"Wait." Sanna follows the girl to the front door. "If I don't shoot, what do I do instead?"

"Just hit as hard as you can." Owena steps outside of the cottage. "Hit until the devil stops moving."

First, she can't see them lying there. Just a herd of wild horses galloping across the fields. They zigzag around the cottages, up the village hills, and toward the resort. But then Sanna sees the first collapsed adult. A woman wearing bleached overalls and a sun hat lies outstretched by the gardens and greenhouses.

Sanna stops to stare at her. Then she reaches for Owena's hand, but the girl pulls her arm away. "I saw it," she says. "Let's keep going."

They make their way around the row of cottages. Owena's marching steps thump against the dry ground. Sanna focuses on listening to their steady tempo, but then her eyes adjust, and she starts picking them out, one by one.

A man sitting on a swing, his head drooping against his shoulder.

A woman on the grass, arm twisted like someone tied a knot in it.

Another man, face swimming in a puddle of blood.

"Are they dead?" Sanna whispers, failing to follow the marching Owena. When Sanna falls to her knees, the rifle drops next to her, making a clicking sound. Shaking and sobbing, Sanna digs her fingers into the dry soil. Owena's footsteps come closer, then stop a few feet away.

"What's wrong?"

Sanna looks up, too surprised to continue crying. Without looking at the unresponsive people around them, Sanna points in the direction of the swing. "Owena, something happened to them."

"I know."

"Something bad."

"Just pretend that they're sleeping." Owena bites her lower lip. "You need to get up, Sanna. We need to keep going."

Sanna continues to shake and gasp for air. "I can't get up. I'm too scared."

Owena stands there, staring at her. "Don't be scared." She seems anxious to keep moving. "Think of happy things."

"Like what?"

Owena pauses and picks up the rifle, hands it to Sanna. "Something fun. Like songs. Or jokes."

"Jokes?"

Owena grabs Sanna's shoulder, pulling as hard as she can. Then they start walking toward the swing, heading to a dirt path that leads to the resort. As they pass the sleeping adults, motionless and silent, Sanna closes her eyes. She thinks hard about any jokes that she knows. The only person she can remember telling jokes is Bill.

"Owena, do you think Bill is dead too?"

"Sleeping. Bill is sleeping."

Sanna swallows the sob in her throat. What were the jokes called, the ones Bill would tell them at breakfast in the hotel's kitchen? Sanna inhales deeply, the memory of Bill's voice in her head.

"Knock, knock," Bill would say.

"Who's there?" Sanna would answer, rolling her eyes but grinning.

"Broken pencil."

"Broken pencil who?"

"Never mind. It's pointless."

The swing is now behind them. It's quiet. Quieter than Sanna remembers it ever being since she left her home in the blue city. The building she had lived in was called the Chip-Center. It wasn't a bad place. Her room had been nice. The big leather chair in it was soft and comfy. She even had friends. Secret friends, too, like the lady who visited behind her window and brought . . .

"Owena, I forgot Mister Bun-Bun. He's still in the cottage!"

The little girl keeps walking up the path. "Well, go back and get him."

Sanna stops by the path, torn between following Owena or going back to save her beloved bunny. What if Mister Bun-Bun is asleep too? The thought is too horrible to be true. Breathing becomes harder and harder. Like an invisible monster is sitting on Sanna's chest. Or a scarf that's wrapped around her throat too tightly. Or when you have a cough, and you're afraid that you'll forget to breathe. What would it be like? Falling asleep like all those adults? Would it hurt?

Sanna sprints after Owena. By the path, more sleeping people rest in awkward-looking positions. She knows them all, and not just by their names. All adults who take care of them. *Took* care of them.

Where are all the children? Are they asleep too? The thought makes Sanna gasp for air. It makes her stomach twist, like she's eaten worms and ants for breakfast. She moves faster on the trail, keeping her watery eyes on Owena's back.

"Knock, knock," Memory-Bill says.

"Who's there?"

"Urine."

"Urine who?"

"Urine trouble, Sanna. If you don't open this door right now!"

The green tarp's corner flaps in the air, partly uncovering the empty pool. As they near the bar area, five dogs run over to the girls, waving their tails and whining. More dogs circle the pool, anxious and restless. Worried barks and whines fill the air.

Sanna kneels down to greet the yellow mutt called Wacko, while Owena walks toward the back door. It's cracked open, and when Sanna looks again, she sees Owena stepping over an unmoving body. Right next to the man's hand, a kitchen knife reflects the sunbeams on its surface. Sanna looks away and buries her face into the dog's long hair.

"*Knock, knock.*"

"*Who's there?*"

"*Oink oink.*"

"*Oink oink who?*"

"*Make up your mind—are you a pig, or an owl?*"

Supporting herself on the doorframe, Sanna steps over the collapsed man, first with her left leg, then her right. The long-haired dog follows her inside, leaping over the body with ease. Owena's heading to the kitchen, seemingly oblivious to the motionless chaos around her. Sanna focuses on the dog's face, blurring the sleepers from her sight. Just the dog and her. The dog, her, and Memory-Bill.

She takes a deep breath, keeps walking.

"*Knock, knock.*"

"*Who's there?*"

"*Figs.*"

"*Figs who?*"

"*Figs the doorbell, it's broken.*"

In the kitchen, Owena circles around, looking under counters and peeking into closets. Sanna wants to help but has no idea what the girl is doing. It takes her awhile to get the question out of her throat where it's stuck. To do both—talk and breathe—seems impossible.

"What are you looking for?" she finally asks Owena, her voice cracking.

"My axe." Owena tilts her head and stares at Sanna, like she should understand as much without her stating the obvious.

"I thought maybe you were looking for your friends?"

"Who?"

"The kids."

Owena nods slowly. "Yes. Those too."

There are about a hundred of them, kids from City of England. The people they saw outside—the sleeping people—were all adults. Where are the kids?

Owena moves through the enormous kitchen, peeking under every surface there is. A couple of chairs are overturned. Sanna fast-walks to them and places them upright again. *Here, I helped*, she thinks, happy to have something to do with her hands. She's just about to follow Owena to the back door when she hears a muffled sob.

"Owena, psst."

Waving her hand, Sanna gestures for the girl to follow her into the main pantry closet. As they open the door, the sound of several gasps fills the air. The room is dark, and it takes a moment for their eyes to adjust.

"Marie?" Owena whispers. "Sarah? Are you here?"

The two girls Owena used to play with down in the valley. They used to be roommates at their previous home. They had left a place called Kinship Care to join Kaarina's adventure. Owena, Sarah, Marie. And Ava—the only Unchipped person among them.

Unchipped, just like me, Sanna thinks. They're not supposed to tap each other in this new home. Because here, it doesn't matter whether you have a chip or not. No one should feel like an outsider. But surely Kaarina wouldn't be mad if she did it now? She has to do it to get help. Right? Sanna squeezes her eyes shut and focuses the way Kaarina once taught her. She taps for Ava. Then Kaarina. Then Bill. Micky. Even the scary Yeti.

No one replies.

Owena clears away buckets and sacks of flour and makes her way all the way to the back of the pantry. There, a green tarp identical to the one in the pool covers old pots and pans, coolers, and broken chairs. She crawls in and helps her friends out of their hiding place. Marie sobs quietly and runs to hug Sanna. They're about the same age, but suddenly Sanna feels years older than Marie.

"I think they're dead," Marie sobs, holding onto Sanna tightly.

"Who is?" Sanna asks. "Have you been outside?"

"No. It's Kaarina. And Yeti." Marie nods at the green tarp. "They're in there. But they're not moving."

Sarah crawls out from the hiding place, and a dozen kids follow her, all with pale, bloodless faces, their eyes stricken with terror. Owena makes her way out last, peeks under the tarp, and turns to Marie. "Where are the rest?"

Marie doesn't let go of Sanna. "I think they're dead," she says again.

"The adults are dead," Owena says, her eyes blinking and face blank. "But where are the kids?"

They're all sobbing now; some shake and bury their faces in their hands. Owena stares at them for a while, blinking rapidly. Then she turns to Sanna, her face calm and horror-free.

"Help me find them."

Sanna looks around, thinking hard. She wants to help. Wants to have something to do, so she can block the sleeping people out of her mind. Where would she go, if this were a game of hide and seek?

Wacko trots in and nudges Sanna's hand. Then he continues into the pantry and sniffs around the tarp, trying to get to where Kaarina and Yeti still lie hidden. Sanna stares at the dog, while Owena's eyes drill into her. The girl's still waiting for an answer. Wacko starts digging at the tarp, causing the corner to flap against the pantry floor.

Sanna inhales sharply, then meets Owena's eyes. "The pool. There's enough room under the tarp for all of them."

Owena blinks twice, then turns to leave the pantry. Wacko follows her out, and the kids follow the dog. Sanna peeks over her shoulder, hoping to see movement under the tarp, but she sees nothing there. The adults are asleep. Even the fearless Kaarina. Even Yeti, who stares at Kaarina when he thinks nobody's watching. He stares like she's Christmas Eve or a birthday cake. Or he did—until he fell asleep among sacks of flour and broken chairs and smelly buckets.

They sit in the deck chairs on the pale concrete of the poolside, wrapped in the fleece blankets that Markus gives them on chilly nights for story time. Now Markus is nowhere to be seen. Owena sits quietly, pouting and deep in thought. Sanna wants to ask her what she's thinking but is too afraid to hear the answer. Owena's weird. Different from everyone else. But Kaarina always says that it's okay to be different, and that everyone should be exactly who they are, and that you should be very careful not to judge anyone. Because you never know what goes on inside their heads. Whatever she meant by that. Maybe it had something to do with the magical chip?

Though she had never heard anyone talk about it until Kaarina did—about heads and judges and being yourself—that's what Sanna's done, ever since they arrived in Iceland. She's been a friend to Mister Bun-Bun and Owena, even though both of them are different and weird and hard to understand. Now, she's forgotten one of her odd friends in the cottage, and the other one is acting very strange—more so than usual. Something about Owena now reminds Sanna of Kaarina. Like Owena's the five-year-old version of the rebel leader; the way she marches and how she suddenly seems to know exactly what to do.

Everyone sits under their blankets, some softly sobbing, most staring at Owena, waiting.

"Where's Markus?" a boy whose name is Jim asks.

"Yeah, and Micky?" someone half-whispers from under his fleece blanket. "I'm getting hungry."

"Shh," Owena hisses. "I need to think."

"What are you thinking?" Marie asks. She sits a few feet away from Owena, wrapped under a single blanket with Sarah.

"I think we're stuck here," Owena says, still pouting, her fingers wandering down the barrel of the rifle that Sanna had carried to the hotel.

"We need to call someone," Sanna says. "Doesn't Ava have a phone? I think I've seen her play with one, when she thought no one was watching."

Owena's frantic eyes drill into Sanna. "Those are the devil's devices. You can't touch them, ever."

Sanna blinks, staring at Owena uncomprehendingly. Some of the kids nod at Owena's words, their eyes wide and scared.

"No, I mean a phone. Like an antique one. Not AR-glasses," Sanna says, hoping that Owena will budge. She's heard Owena talk about the AR-glasses before, how she's convinced they will hurt you, maybe turn you into a slobbery, slimy monster. At least that's what the devil looks like in her mind.

"All those things. They are bad. We can't call anyone. We're stuck here, just us."

Owena's words create louder sobs under the blankets. Some of the kids hug each other, their faces swollen and smudged with tears. Sanna should do something. Why aren't the older kids saying anything? Why isn't anyone comforting them?

"Knock, knock," says Sanna. They all stare at her, a hush falling over them.

"Knock, knock," she says again and sits taller. A hundred pairs of eyes stare at her in wonder.

"Who's there?" someone finally whispers from under their blanket.

"Cow says."

They blink and stare, some of their lips forming the letter O.

"Cow says who?" Marie finally asks.

"No, cow says moo!"

Giggles and brief laughter fill the poolside. It makes the dogs circle around them happily, wagging their tails and licking their faces. The kids laugh more. Then a steady chattering begins, as they all start sharing their knock-knock jokes with one another.

Sanna gets on all fours and makes her way to Owena. The girl is still deep in thought, now facing away from the others, staring at the mountainside. Sanna sits close to her but doesn't wrap her arm around her. Something tells her Owena wouldn't like that.

"Why are you so quiet?" she asks.

But Owena doesn't answer. She closes her eyes, and her lips turn into a thin line. Several minutes pass before Sanna realizes what she's trying to do.

"Owena, that won't work. You can't tap the adults."

Finally, she opens her eyes and turns to look at Sanna. "Why not?"

"Because you don't have that thing in your brain."

"What thing?"

"A microchip."

"But you do?"

"I do."

"But it doesn't work?"

"It doesn't. That's why I'm able to tap people."

Owena frowns, still staring at Sanna. "I don't get it."

"Don't worry," Sanna says and smiles. "I don't really get it either."

"Have you tried to talk to them?"

"Kaarina and the other adults? I have. They won't talk back to me. I don't think they ever will . . . " Sanna's voice cracks in the middle of her sentence.

"Because they're asleep," Owena then says, turning her gaze back to the mountains.

They sit there a long time, Sanna half-listening to the knock-knock jokes behind her by the pool. Wacko jogs over and dives under Sanna's arm. He sits with them quietly. Then another dog, Tiny, joins them, pushing her body against Owena's. The little girl doesn't turn to look at the dog by her side but puts her arm around him without taking her gaze from whatever she sees on the horizon. Slowly, her fingers caress the short dog hair. Sometimes late at night, Sanna can hear Owena talk to them—the dogs, never another kid, or any of the adults. It's like she tolerates people around her but doesn't really care if she's alone or not. But the dogs she likes, Sanna has noticed.

First, it's just a dull, rhythmic thump in the distance, a sound that might as well be a trick of the wind or a herd of wild horses tearing the white plastic from a hay bale in the barnyard. But then, they see the flying machines rising above the mountains. Owena stiffens next to Sanna, still staring. She doesn't say a word. None of the other kids seem to have noticed the helicopters in the distance.

Sanna narrows her eyes, trying to see better. She's seen helicopters before. At the Chip-Center, where she used to live. The doctor that took care of her would let her see them every weekend, on the roof, coming in and taking off. There was not much to do at the Chip-Center, so the copters were a highlight of Sanna's week. They were much like these ones, making their way to the resort. Sanna keeps her eyes on them. When the nearest one comes close enough for the rest of the kids to see the blades and hear their chuff-chuff-chuff and the whine of the engines, Sanna sees the logo on the side. It's the same helicopter she used to stare at, back in the blue city. The Happiness-Program logo on its side shines with a neon-blue light.

"Knock, knock," she whispers to Owena. The girl stares at the machines, with an expression on her face that could be horror or curiosity or relief. It's very hard to know with Owena.

"Who's there?" the little girl asks. She's holding her breath, Sanna can tell. Why is she so bothered by helicopters and phones?

"Doctor."

"Doctor who?"

The blue helicopter lands between the resort and the village. The kids sit motionless, no one says a word. Most of them have never seen anything but birds in the sky.

Owena reaches for Sanna's arm, squeezing it tight. "Sanna, doctor who?" she asks.

Sanna reaches for Owena's hand and closes it tight between her palms.

"Doctor Laura Solomon."

6
LAURA

April 2089
East-Land, City of Finland

PROLOGUE
2085, CITY OF CHINA

"Dear friends, colleagues, and business associates. Welcome."

Applause. It soothes her ears, caresses her ego, makes her lift her chin an inch. The smooth fabric on her white doctor's coat rustles gently against the microphone attached to her lapel. She adjusts the device, then pauses to take in the audience. So many of them here today. All eager to hear her vision for humanity's second chance.

"Most of you know my mother, Marjaana Salonen, who was unfortunately unable to be here with us today. As of today, June first, 2085, my beloved mother has stepped away from the Solomon Foundation, resigning in good spirits and good health."

More applause. Sure, her mother deserves some praise, too. Without Pharma Salonen and her mother's childish plans to heal and cure every single person on this rotting planet, Laura wouldn't be standing here today. Visionary. Powerful. Fearless. *In charge.*

"Happiness and the future. These two words may seem incompatible today, as we witness all the horrifying forms The Great Affliction is taking." She steps to the side, her hands folded in front of her midriff. "The future. What does it hold?"

"Starvation!" someone yells from the audience.

"Mass murder!" another participant adds.

"Suicide!"

Laura cocks her head, walking calmly across the stage. Eyes fixed on the floor, fingertips tapping against one another, she frowns and takes her time before continuing.

"Isn't that how the world already looks today?"

The audience stays quiet.

"So, let's put the future aside for a moment. Let's talk about happiness. What does this word mean to you?"

"Peace!"

"Secure jobs!"

"Safety for our children!"

Laura stops and turns to face the audience. She opens her arms, palms facing forward.

"Okay. Now let's put the two together. Happiness. The future. What if I told you these two words don't need to be mutually exclusive?" She takes a step forward, pauses for a reassuring smile. "What if these two things could be one and the same?"

A low murmur. No clapping. They don't believe her. But Laura knew they wouldn't. She watches her audience closely. Some fold their arms across their chests. Some lean closer to get a better look at the screen where Doctor Solomon—the person whom they've all come to see and hear—gives her best performance. And how easy it all is. Reassuring body language. Well-articulated words. Strategic pauses. She could do this in her sleep. She'll never feel more comfortable in her own skin.

"Now, I'll give you another power couple. Mind mapping and AR-programming. The latest progress we've made on the corpus callosum bridges is phenomenal. The Solomon Foundation will soon be the first in the world to successfully upload a human mind into a computer. How many of you are familiar with our whole-brain emulation trials?"

A hundred hands. Maybe more. Laura already knows that those who sit with their arms folded will also be familiar with her work. Why else would they be here today? Fifty thousand nuyuan seems like a high price to come and sit in a conference room just for soy-sausage sandwiches and instant coffee—even for the wealthy.

"In the last seminar, we introduced the latest devices our team has perfected: the regenerative healing capsule and the chipping helmet. Thanks to my mother, we are now able to use these devices to heal those who suffer from nearly any injury or disability. Let the blind see again, and the deaf hear."

This time, the applause is louder. Half of the audience stands up, nodding and whooping. Even those with folded arms now stare at Laura with newfound curiosity.

That's right, my dear peasants, she thinks. *Bow down.*

Patiently, she waits for the fanfare to cease. Then she continues her steady circling on the stage. She snaps her fingers and waits while two men roll in a hand truck carrying a stasis capsule. The pod lands on the stage with a dull *thump*. Laura reaches in and takes out a chipping helmet with multiple wires protruding from it.

"Just like happiness and the future," she says, "mind mapping and AR go hand in hand. We've already had tremendous success with mind remapping when treating PTSD patients. However, even though we are now able to erase specific memories and replace them with new ones, our experts still have a long way to go before we can fully recover a damaged mind, or prevent it from ever becoming damaged in the first place. Our work is a constant race with mental illness, drug abuse, violence, and record-low fertility rates that plague our world. People are dying faster than we can heal them. People are suffering and that's why they're taking justice into their own hands."

"Banish drug addicts!"

"Lock up the rebels and outlaws!"

"No more guns!"

Laura raises her free hand, the other one holding the helmet. The shouting ends, and the audience sits back down to listen.

"I agree. And to solve these massive issues, we need ambitious tools." She raises the helmet to eye level, investigating it closely with a confident smile on her face. "For our new AR-society to succeed, we need to develop the human mind and its capabilities to levels far beyond what was considered acceptable in the past."

A long pause. Laura keeps her eyes on the helmet. For a moment, she imagines her mother's face in it. The deep wrinkles around her closed eyes. Eyes that had never been anything but soft and forgiving. But that's the problem with Laura's mother. *Softness*. With her lukewarm attitude and the way she'd always take a step back when it was time to take two forward, Marjaana Salonen is a thing of the past. Let her finally get some rest. Tucked away, in storage for the time being. Until Laura finally finishes what her fragile mother never could.

"We've come a long way from just reading the mind with nanoparticles. Understanding how the brain works without having to slice it into layers has pushed us well beyond recording dreams and entering databases with our minds. Enter microchip technology. Intelligence amplification has never seen a brighter future than it does today."

Laura lowers the helmet, holding on with two hands. Her smile fades as she stands tall in front of her audience. Chest broad, chin high.

"Dear friends, colleagues, and business associates." She looks down, closes her eyes. The long pause creates static in the air. No one moves, no one dares to breathe. Laura looks up, her eyes drilling into the crowd.

"I give you the Happiness-Program."

CHAPTER 1
INSIDE A GLASS BOX

Cheeks flushed, fingers wandering on the smooth surface of the AR-glasses, Laura sits in her gaming chair. The simulation she's returning from is not the kind that most people choose to visit. The past. Her past. Five years back, she had left Iceland and traveled to a conference held in City of China, knowing that she was about to change the world. That day, with her mother finally set aside, she had taken full control of it all. The Solomon Foundation. Her life. *Everyone's* lives.

And today, five years later, here she is, still changing the world. And her mother, Mrs. Salonen, still can't stop her, though now her whereabouts are unknown, since she had disappeared from what Laura had thought was a secure location in Iceland before her men got there. Maybe she's still out there, living her final days alone at the empty resort.

Maybe she's dead.

Laura shakes her head, ridding herself of restless and useless thoughts. Thoughts like these are new to her. She can fathom no reason for them to exist. Everything is going her way. Her mission to create a new type of world—an advanced human race—is about to become reality. It's not a matter of years anymore, it's a matter of months, weeks, and days. She shouldn't feel drained or worried. There's no one standing in her way, no one slowing her down.

"Open window. Start clear-sky-sunset. Mountain-view."

A late-April evening in City of Finland opens before her eyes. Then the pixels take over, changing the scenery to a sunset on a mountainside. City of California? City of Spain? She can't quite tell which image the CS has chosen for the window of her penthouse apartment above the Chip-Center.

Hand on a sherry bottle, she chooses a glass from the table next to her and pours herself a drink. Saluting the fake sunset, she drinks more than a sip. It's been a profitable day. In the lab and outside of it. The city is thriving again, with people eager to work and continue their lives in the AR-reality like nothing ever happened. Because nothing did happen—in their Chipped minds. Kaarina's shenanigans in Iceland had been going on for far too long, but Laura had finally put a stop to it. And she'd done it by simply pressing a button.

The Chipped she can control. The Chipless kids from Kinship Care have all had their operations now. If she could only find the right code to tweak the Unchipped brain in the same way . . .

A knock on the door. Nurse Saarinen peeks in.

Laura turns her chair toward the door, her body tingling after the simulation. Or maybe it's the sherry kicking in. "Yes?"

"Sorry to bother you, Laura." Nothing in Nurse Saarinen's voice sounds apologetic. Some days Laura wonders if the woman is using the chip technology to tweak her own mind, to update her processing power and numb down the parts that feel. Nurse Saarinen thinks and acts in a unique way, and it's always been hard to read between her lines. Like the fact that she wants people to call her a nurse, when her education, knowledge, and experience have honed her skillset and talent much closer to that of a neurosurgeon. "It's her. Again."

Laura sighs and puts down the sherry. With one finger she draws a line on the edge of the glass. "Another nightmare?"

"I'm afraid so."

She picks up the glass and empties it in one gulp. Why she's not storming toward the bedroom at the end of her penthouse apartment is beyond her.

"I can just administer her another pill . . ."

"No!" The harshness of Laura's voice surprises them both. It's unlike her to raise her voice or react to Nurse Saarinen with emotion. Maybe she should check her hormone levels at the lab? She clears her throat, gets up from the chair. "No," she says with a softer voice. "I'll take care of it."

Blanket pulled up to cover most of her face, the girl stares at Laura, eyes wide. A nightlight throws long shadows around the bedroom. A teddy bear and a porcelain doll stare down from the shelves. The doll looks more like a corpse than a toy meant for children. Laura sits on the edge of the bed, staring at the evil-looking doll with its pale skin and empty eyes.

"Do you hate it too?"

Laura rips her gaze from the toy and looks at the girl with long, black hair.

"Do I hate what, dear?"

"The doll. It's creepy, isn't it?"

Frowning, Laura stares at Sanna's face. Then she gives her a little smile. "I think you're right. The doll is kind of sinister. Where did it come from?"

"That woman."

"What woman?"

"With the voice."

"Nurse Saarinen?"

Sanna nods. "Sometimes when she talks, it hurts my ears."

Laura smiles. The girl makes her feel helpless, somehow inadequate. Building a better world, modifying humanity, healing a society after war . . . it all comes naturally to Laura. But enter a kid—her own child—with wide, innocent eyes and startling questions, and suddenly, she's clueless.

Laura gets up and walks to the shelf. She takes down the doll and wipes the rough hair off its face. Sanna lowers the blanket and supports her weight by leaning into her shoulders. She tilts her head and blinks her eyes rapidly.

"You want me to get rid of her?" Laura asks.

Sanna stares at her, pink lips pouting as she ponders the question. "But why?"

"You said you hate her. That she's creepy."

The girl nods firmly. "I do."

"Okay, then. The doll should go."

Laura turns to leave the room. As she nears the open door, a frantic voice stops her. "Wait!"

Holding the doll in her hands, Laura turns around. Suddenly, she feels way too exhausted to follow her daughter's strange thought process.

"She can stay. The doll. Just put her back on the shelf."

Laura cocks her head. The sherry has kicked in, making her legs tired. When she thinks of it, it's not just her legs that need rest. It's her arms and hands. Stomach and lungs. Brain and mind. Ever since the Unchipped were shipped from Iceland to their cities of origin, she's been working twenty-four-seven.

"But I don't understand," Laura says, placing the doll back on the shelf despite her doubts. "So you *do* like the doll?"

Sanna shakes her head no.

"That's what I thought. So why would you want her to stay?"

Sanna lies back down and pulls the blanket up to her chin. Still pouting, she looks up at the toys on the wall and says, "Just because I don't like her, it doesn't mean she's bad."

Laura shoves her hands into the pockets of her robe. She's lost all words.

"Just leave the doll alone, Doctor Solomon," Sanna says. She turns her back on Laura and pulls the blanket over her head. "I don't want any more faces disappearing from around me while I sleep."

Shortening her footsteps so the girl can tag along is harder than Laura would have thought. The Chip-Center is turning smaller and smaller in the distance as they near the city center. Her vision slightly blurred, Sanna looks around the city in awe. She can't see the half of it—just the billboards and the tile roads—but it doesn't stop her from spinning around, her neck outstretched to take it all in. Should Laura have given her so many painkillers? The Unchipped brain isn't suited for roaming around the city. Laura can't wait for the day when she can fix Sanna's malfunctioning implant. Maybe then she'll tell the girl that she is more than just her doctor.

Once the girl is properly chipped, things will get better. Easier. Sanna could finally join other kids at the Happiness-Program's AR school and receive an education. Become someone important. Someone with a bright future and a high social rank. Just like Laura, or maybe . . . *better* than Laura. But as long as the girl is Unchipped, none of this is available to her.

As an Unchipped, she's just one test subject among all the others.

The AR-glasses buzz against Laura's forehead. It's business hours, so she should pick up the call. Especially now, as multiple new stasis capsules are humming to life. So far, so good. All the people in the capsules have remained in medically induced comas while Nurse Saarinen's crew perfects the chipping process. Not that the Unchipped can be appropriately chipped. But they can be contained and put to work, whether they know that they're working or not. Without the processing power from those who sleep in the stasis capsules, none of the cities could run for a single day.

Only Sanna and the young Owena remain outside the basement and the lab, where the rest of the captured rebels now rest. Owena is the last of the Chipless Kinship Care children, and her operation is scheduled for tomorrow. Sanna will need more time. Operating on an Unchipped brain is always a risk, and during rechipping trials many adults have experienced complications. But there's more than that, when it comes to children. A child's rapidly developing brain is harder to map and modify than an adult's fully developed prefrontal cortex.

But the fact that rechipping a young Unchipped girl would probably take a lot more time and effort than fixing an adult Unchipped person is not the only reason Laura is hesitant to push Sanna to get rechipped: She wants it to be Sanna's own idea.

With one finger pointing at a tall building up ahead, Sanna turns to Laura. "And what's that?"

"That's a Vertical Farming-Center. Where all our food comes from."

"How about that?" She points to another building that glows with a blue light.

"The Nursery. That's where . . ." Laura stops to clear her throat. Why is it so hard for her to just tell Sanna the truth? "That's where you were born. My dear, it's not like you've never seen the city before. Have you really forgotten so much while you were away?"

"No, I remember," Sanna says. "It's just that it all looks different. Now that I've seen so many other places around the world." She stops to think, a faint crease on her smooth forehead. "Have you been to City of Serbia, Doctor Solomon?"

"Yes, I have."

"How about City of England?"

"Not for a long time, I haven't."

"But you've been there?"

"Yes, dear. I've been there."

"And Iceland? Oh, oh! Have you seen the wild horsies?"

Laura forces a smile. "Yes. They are beautiful." Iceland is the last thing she wants to talk about with Sanna.

They keep walking, Laura stepping on the blue tiles and Sanna walking beside her on a concrete path. A steady buzzing against her skull prompts Laura to shove the AR-glasses into the breast pocket of her lab coat. Sanna's eyes fixate on the pocket, then turn to Laura.

"Can I see?"

"What, the glasses?"

The girl nods, her black hair barely moving around her pale face.

"I'm afraid that's not a great idea, my dear. But soon."

"Why not now?"

"The glasses will hurt you, dear." Like a reflex, Laura turns to look in the direction of the Chip-Center. She's not used to being away from it this long. Neither is Sanna, though it doesn't seem to bother her as much. The extra blockers in her system work better than Laura expected them to. "But I'm about to fix that, dear. If you'd like me to. Wouldn't it be neat to see all the colors and lights and holograms?"

Sanna shrugs. Then she turns and keeps walking. Where are they going exactly? Where is Laura to go with an Unchipped child that can't enjoy anything the city has to offer? The simulation center wouldn't work, nor the AR-zoo. They could get vegan ice cream, but the MintChipDelight is in the middle of an AR-mall ablaze with neon lights and CS technology. Sanna would be sick before they got through the revolving door.

"Where are all the animals?" Sanna has stopped to stare at a tree across the concrete park. The old oak tree is located between the hologram bases on the ground. Laura's never noticed it before. Whatever trees and plants remain in the city are usually camouflaged by the flickering lights and messages. As rare as it is for her to walk around the city, it's even rarer for her to do so without AR-glasses on her face.

"The animals are different here, dear."

"Different how?"

"Well, you can't see them without the glasses."

The girl frowns. She hasn't stopped staring at the oak tree. "So if I had the glasses, I could see animals around? Right now?"

"Yes, dear."

"What kind?"

"I'm sorry?"

"What animals would I see?"

Laura blinks, staring at Sanna's wide eyes. The innocent look on her face troubles Laura, makes her feel uneasy, though she has no idea why. This is her daughter. Her flesh and blood. Yet every time they're together, Laura feels as if she's trying to solve a puzzle with worn and damaged pieces. They simply won't fit.

She digs out the AR-glasses and puts them on. She looks around. Happiness-Pill commercials. Holograms of herself announcing the new peace in the city. Billboards advertising the newest 3D-printed and home-delivered dish of vegan mozzarella sticks.

People walk by, wearing expensive clothing and perfect makeup and thousand-CC haircuts. A man dressed in a navy-blue suit approaches them, his sharp jaw and bedroom eyes looking straight into Laura. She reaches for the glasses and pulls them off. The same man now wears blue coveralls, his thin hair swirling in the wind. Puffy eyes and bad skin tell the tale of his greasy diet. Most people in the city are shaped like pears, both women and men. Laura pushes the glasses back onto her face and nods at the man. He nods back, flashing a perfect pearly smile.

A woman strolls past them, her curves swaying from side to side. Her long, thick hair dances around the golden dress she's wearing with matching high heels. Just the sight of the shoes makes Laura's back hurt. She takes off the glasses and sees a middle-aged woman dressed in blue coveralls. Her close-shaved head is slightly pink, her skull burned in the midday sun.

Glasses back on, Laura does her best to ignore it all and scan the surroundings for something she usually wouldn't be interested in seeing. Animals. At first, there's nothing there for her to see. Then—a neon-green butterfly flits around the oak tree. Then another. A third one. Then a rabbit the size of a small dog. Its floppy ears bouncing, the digi-critter jumps along the tile road, making its way to Sanna, then stands up on its hind legs.

"There's a rabbit," Laura says, nodding at the AR-creature next to Sanna's feet.

"Where?"

"Right next to you. It's climbing up against your thigh."

For a moment, Sanna's face lights up with excitement. Then the frown returns, and her lips turn into a slight pout.

"What's wrong?" Laura asks. "I thought you liked bunnies."

"I do."

"Then what is it? Are you upset that you can't see this one?" Laura walks over and kneels down next to Sanna. She runs her hand over the AR-bunny's floppy ears.

"It's not real."

Laura hesitates. "No . . . " she says slowly. "Not real, but better."

The girl cocks her head. "What do you mean, better?"

"Well, first of all, they have no smell to them. And you don't need to feed them or look after them. They can't attack you or cause damage to their surroundings. There's simply no harm or bother in having them around."

"Yeah . . . " Sanna stretches her reply. "But they're not real."

Frustration washes over Laura. The sleepless nights have started to take their toll. She makes a mental note to check her serotonin and dopamine levels as soon as she's back at the Chip-Center.

Laura shrugs. "They look real enough to me."

"But you just said they're not."

"I know what I said." Laura's patience is running low. "You're just too young to understand."

The girl shakes her head. "You said they don't smell like anything. And I know what a real bunny smells like because I had one. His name was Mister Bun-Bun," the girl says. "And I lost him when Niina died."

Laura looks up and stares at Sanna. How the hell does one have a pet bunny while running around the world with a rebel crew? Maybe she's lying. Kids do that, don't they?

Sanna kicks a small rock on the concrete road. "Can we just go back to the Chip-Center now?"

She sidesteps away from Laura, nearing the oak tree where a dozen invisible butterflies dance between the fake leaves. Sanna turns and starts to walk back toward the Chip-Center.

Laura follows the girl. "But there's so much more to see. Aren't you curious?"

Sanna keeps walking. "Not really," she murmurs.

"Why not?"

"I can't explain it to you." She tucks her chin against her chest. "And even if I did, you probably wouldn't understand."

Her fingers run smoothly on the invisible keyboard. Multiple screens in front of Laura show charts and calculations, X-rays and brain scans, medical files of fifteen different test subjects, some currently the Chip-Center's tenants, some stored away downstairs. She's the last one in the lab. Everyone else has left, gone home to enjoy another evening of government-issued pill-high, the newest show on the wellness-channel, and a vegan dinner delivered to their doorstep. The curfew started hours ago.

Footsteps in the corridor. Laura doesn't turn around to see who's come to snap her back into this reality. The reality where she needs to drink, eat, and tuck her daughter in for the night. Not that Sanna needs her care. The girl is far beyond needing a mother, despite her tender age of ten.

A knock on the door. "Laura? It's way past midnight," says Nurse Saarinen's slightly cracked voice.

"I knew that, thanks."

"Did you?"

She didn't. She's lost all sense of time while working on figuring out the difference between an Unchipped brain and a Chipped brain. She sighs and gets up from the stool. Stretching her arms, she can't stifle a long yawn.

"She's sleeping?"

Nurse Saarinen shrugs. "Last I checked."

"No nightmares?"

Another shrug.

"I wonder if the blockers are messing with her head. Giving her bad dreams."

Nurse Saarinen doesn't say anything but gives Laura a funny look. Amusement? Annoyance? It's hard to say with her. The woman is like a robot.

Laura walks to a workspace next to hers, taps on the CS control, and swipes to the left. Her mind gives the orders without her needing to think about what she's doing. She's lived in the programs and control panels of this database for years now. To be apart from it feels like losing a limb or a portion of her brain. She's still recovering from her trip to the city earlier in the day.

The camera icon flickers, and she presses the play button. A dim light, a teddy bear, and a pale doll with a dead face appear in her view. Nurse Saarinen puts on her AR-glasses and joins Laura. Together they stare at the girl, sleeping peacefully under the blankets.

"Did you tell her yet?" Nurse Saarinen asks.

Laura rubs her temples, wishing her most trusted colleague knew how to read a room. That she'd have a small piece of empathy left in her brain. If there was any in the first place. But then again—would she be the genius she is? Maybe the fact that Nurse Saarinen doesn't care about mothers and daughters and family reunions is what makes her so incredibly efficient.

Laura shakes her head. "I guess I'm not sure how."

The girl turns over and rolls onto her other side, still sound asleep.

"We have everything ready. We can proceed as soon as tomorrow, if you like."

The chipping. She's been talking about trying to fix Sanna's chip, not about Laura telling the girl she's her long-lost mother. Ever since the Unchipped rebels were brought back from Iceland, Nurse Saarinen has been anxious to try her latest discovery about adjusting the implant in an Unchipped brain. She tells Laura that operating on a child should have a far higher success rate than operating on a fully developed brain.

"We're not . . ." Laura's voice breaks. She clears her throat and keeps her eyes on the camera view. "We're not quite ready for the operation yet." Nurse Saarinen gives her a serious look but doesn't say anything.

The girl starts kicking in her sleep, clutching the white sheets in her clenched fists. Laura frowns and leans closer to see better. If only she could enter Sanna's mind. The way she could if the girl was Chipped. Then she'd understand this. The nightmares, the questions, her undying fascination with animals.

She could record the bad dreams, maybe erase whatever memory triggers them.

The scream pierces the silence, and Laura hastily takes off the AR-glasses. Nurse Saarinen hasn't winced. A dull expression on her face, she stares at the dreaming girl. Then she shrugs and turns to look at Laura.

"She did say something the other day. When I woke her up from one of these things."

"Things?"

Nurse Saarinen waves her hand in the air, looking for the right word. "These . . . fits. Nightmares."

"What did she say?"

Nurse Saarinen takes off her glasses. "It's not going to make you happy."

"Just spit it out. Did she ask for something?"

"Yes."

"Well, go on." Laura gestures for her to keep talking. "What does she need?"

"It's not *what*, but *who*."

Laura feels dizzy. It's not going to be the girl's mother Sanna wants by her side. A parent to comfort her after a bad dream is not something she grew up with. Laura is of no importance in the girl's life. To Sanna, she's nothing but an odd doctor who brought her back to a city she once left to go on an adventure.

Laura sucks in her lower lip and takes a deep breath. "Who did she ask for?"

"That long-haired Chipped." Nurse Saarinen waves her hand above her short red hair. She's distracted, placing her AR-glasses on and off her face. "What's his face," she mumbles.

"Nyman?" Laura says, surprise knocking her head back. "She asked for Markus?"

Nurse Saarinen snaps her fingers. "That's him. Yes."

Laura puts the AR-glasses on and shuts down the camera and the control panel. Then she walks out of the lab and waits until Nurse Saarinen has followed her into the blue-lit corridor. "Well, let's go see Mister Nyman, then."

She switches off the light and closes the door. Together they walk to the elevator, but instead of pressing the penthouse button, Nurse Saarinen chooses the lowest blue button with no icon on it.

❋

The capsules hum around her as Laura makes her way through the basement. She keeps her gaze fixed forward, checking the neon signs for section numbers. Nurse Saarinen has stayed in the operating station, checking the chipping helmet one more time for Owena's operation in the morning.

The AR-glasses buzz slightly against Laura's face. A white arrow appears in front of her, telling her to take a right turn, then continue four meters forward and take another turn until she arrives at her desti-nation. She barely ever visits the glass rooms. The prisoners and test subjects who are kept outside the stasis capsules are Nurse Saarinen's crew's responsibil-ity, and the glass rooms are separated from the rest of the basement, away from curious eyes.

The blue tiles flicker on as she makes her way to a glass box with a bed, writing desk, bookshelf, and hardwood floor. The other boxes are dark. Only one tenant is up, sitting in the corner of his new home, staring into space. Laura stands in front of the glass, clears her throat. The man keeps staring, doesn't meet her gaze.

"How are you tonight, Markus?"

The man wets his lips but doesn't say a word.

"The food okay? You getting enough exercise time?"

Nothing.

He's been in the glass room since the Unchipped shipment arrived from Iceland. The rebels with malfunctioning brain chips now rest in the stasis capsules a couple of rows down. Those marked as test subjects are stationed in the glass boxes. Markus is to be fully scanned and researched after his recent experience, when he was forced to attack and kill the other rebels around him while in an unconscious state.

While he was under Laura's control, Markus killed a young Unchipped girl named Ava. Most of the other kids survived the attack, which is okay; Laura only needed a few to send out a message. The rebels need to stop. Any unmonitored life outside the cities needs to come to an end. She can't have any more loose ends out there, not if she's to create a more advanced society with no weak links left to ruin it.

"What do you want, Solomon?"

The uncharacteristic coldness of Markus's tone startles Laura.

"I'm just checking up on you."

"In the middle of the night? It must be, what, two a.m.?"

Laura takes off her AR-glasses and gives Markus a smile. "Something like that." Hands crossed behind her back, Laura walks calmly by the glass wall that separates her from the man. It's strange to think that such a favored citizen of City of Finland could have fallen for a woman so far below his own social class.

"What can I say? I'm a night owl."

"Figures," the man mumbles. When he looks up at Laura, she's taken aback by the hostile glare. But then it's gone, as quickly as it appeared.

"What figures?"

"You. Having trouble sleeping at night."

This arrogance is new. Markus used to be one of the highest-ranking tenants in the city. His social rank was so good that, unlike most people, he was granted a promotion and a place of his own even though he hadn't found a companion. Most of the people in the city are single, but some have been able to recreate what used to be called marriage, now called the Chip-Bond.

Children are still a product of the Nursery-Center, something that will hopefully change as the years roll by, and the memory and behavior augmentation technology progresses. Soon Laura should be able to selectively trigger brain sections in charge of adrenaline, dopamine, serotonin, oxytocin, and vasopressin—the mix that people before The Great Affliction would have called *love*. People would procreate again. Having functioning Chip-Bonds would further help Laura organize and control those who live inside the stone wall and beyond. The brain chemistry of happiness. The final stroke in her master plan.

"Are you just going to stand there grinning like a maniac?"

Markus's words snap Laura out of her trance.

"What?"

"Care to share what you're doing here? Surely you're not worried about my lack of REM sleep."

"Well, dear." Laura nods toward the ceiling. "You and I are not the only ones who have trouble sleeping at night."

"Oh, I'm sure your minions up there in their cozy little apartments are troubled too. Let me guess, they need a sizable pile of colorful pills to get any shuteye?" Markus stands up and walks to the glass wall, now facing Laura. The blueness of his eyes is striking—even when he's not controlled by the implant inside his Chipped brain. "Why should I care?"

Laura shrugs. "Because I know you do."

He lifts his chin an inch. It's like all of Kaarina's arrogance has rubbed off on this man, usually such a pleasant individual. Laura curses the day the Unchipped woman walked into her city and met the innocent Markus.

"I know you care because the one who's tormented by nightmares is Sanna."

Leaning against the door, arms crossed on her chest, Laura stares at Markus's back. He's leaning over Sanna's bed, his ear close to Sanna so he can hear her whispering. Every now and then, Markus leans back and murmurs something to the girl. Laura drops the AR-glasses in front of her eyes to check the time. This reunion has lasted for twenty-five minutes. How can the two have this much to talk about?

She clears her throat. When Markus looks over his shoulder, Laura taps the back of her wrist and nods at the door. Markus turns back to Sanna and keeps murmuring. The girl sits up and wraps her arms around Markus, gives him a long hug. The Chipped man hugs her back and then smooths her black hair, tangled after her restless night.

When Markus nears the door, Laura smiles at Sanna and turns off the light. In the dim glow of her nightlight, the girl dives back under the blanket. Laura closes the door silently behind them.

"Well?"

Markus stops and turns to face Laura. "Well, what? You took her from her family. Brought her back into this . . . this . . . prison. Separated her from everyone she trusts and loves." Markus scoffs and continues to walk toward the elevator. "No wonder she has nightmares."

Laura follows him, sees Nurse Saarinen waiting by the lifts. Dark circles below her eyes tell a tale of sleepless nights spent working on Laura's vision. When she sees Laura and Markus approaching, she raises her hand to let Laura know she'll take it from here. Laura reaches for Markus's shoulder to stop him. "Wait."

The man stops and sidesteps to break free of her grasp. "What now? Sanna's good. At least for tonight."

"That's what I wanted to ask you . . ." Laura's voice goes hoarse at the end of her sentence. She clears her throat and lowers her voice so only Markus can hear. "But what about tomorrow night?"

"What about tomorrow night?"

"You know what I mean." Laura leans closer to Markus. She's surprised when he doesn't move away. "How do I help her feel more . . ."

"Comfortable? At home? Peaceful?"

"Yes. All of that."

Markus takes a moment to investigate Laura's face. Then he scoffs and gives her a smile that doesn't reach his blue eyes. "You need to bring back Mister Bun-Bun. Unless you've already killed him too." He turns and walks to the elevators.

The rabbit. So Sanna hadn't lied, she actually had a pet bunny. If Laura's men found the animal, it would now be either dead or in the lab, stored away for testing and experimentation. Give her a pet . . . of course. Why didn't she think of that?

"Of course I haven't killed the rabbit." Laura looks up, her mind now at ease. "No matter what you think of me, I'm not that . . ." She doesn't know how to end her own sentence.

Insensitive?

Cruel?

Evil?

But she doesn't need to finish her thought. Markus is already in the elevator, dropping back into the depths where his glass prison cell sits waiting for him.

It's four a.m. now, and Laura is nowhere near to getting any sleep. Nurse Saarinen will wake up in an hour. The chipping crew will gather downstairs and begin the operation to implant Owena's chip. If the newest coding works, the little girl will be one of the Chipped and free to live outside the Chip-Center's walls. And hopefully, once Sanna sees her old friend getting an upgrade to an improved version of herself, she'll be up for trying to repair her chip as well.

With her daughter on her side at last, Laura will have it all. A plan. The team and technology to make it happen. Full control of everything and everyone remaining on the planet. With Kaarina shut down and stored in a capsule downstairs, even the rebels can't stand in her way.

"Or so you. Think."

Laura sits up and jumps off the bed in a split second. The voice is too sudden and too clear to have been her imagination. And it doesn't belong to her. Did she fall asleep without even knowing it?

"You're not. Asleep. This isn't. A dream."

She cups her head between her hands. What is going on? Who is this?

"Hello. Old friend."

She knows this voice. The speech impediment.

"Margaret?"

"Did you. Miss. Me?"

This can't be. She must be dreaming. The Unchipped are the ones who suffer from this kind of disturbing glitch in the CS. Not the Chipped. Not her, the person who created it all.

"Why are you inside my head?"

Margaret's laughter booms softly against Laura's skull. Pacing around the bedroom, Laura sits down on the gaming chair, just to get up again. She holds onto her head and waits for a reply.

It doesn't come. The voice has fallen quiet.

Laura perches on the bed, dizzy and out of breath. It's like someone's attacking her from within. An invisible enemy. Locked in, out of reach. It must be her lack of sleep, playing tricks with her auditory cortex. A simple burn out. Exhaustion.

Her hand fumbles for the AR-glasses. Maybe the Meditation-Channel will help. Usually, that's not something she tends to go for, but her mind has clearly fallen over some mental edge she didn't even know existed. Rest. That's all she needs. Tomorrow things will go back to normal again.

"You mean. Today. Don't you?"

Laura jumps back to her feet.

"What?"

"Well. It's almost. Five. In the. Morning."

Her hands press around her head, fingertips drilling into her temples. "This is not happening."

"Okay."

"You're not real."

"Mm."

"Just stop! This isn't happening! How the hell did you hack my chip?"

Laura rips at her hair, holding her breath. Listening, she turns and looks around the room. As if the voice she's hearing might take physical form at any moment. But there's no one there.

"I can see. Why you'd be. So confused. Laura."

She crashes down on her knees.

"All this. Time. You thought. You were the only. One who. Could access. Minds."

CHAPTER 2
THE UNITED INLAND

She fingers the AR-glasses in her lab coat pocket. The elevator glides silently down toward the lab. Feeling off after not getting a minute of sleep, Laura focuses on her breathing. It's hard. She takes a deep breath. Her chest feels heavy, her head dizzy and muddled. Contrary to her usual practice, she decides to take a hefty dose of sleeping pills tonight.

The elevator door opens. The lab is buzzing. Here the scientists are working to improve the augmented reality, the simulations, the mind mapping, the brain emulation trials, and the pills that help people feel more at ease while they learn to cope in their new world. *A better world*, Laura reminds herself while walking toward the testing area.

Miniature versions of the glass rooms—like the room where Markus now lives—are stacked on top of one another. Most of the boxes are empty; they don't really need animals for testing these days. A snake with a zigzag pattern, a dozen mice, three rats—and one black and white rabbit. Sanna's rabbit.

The scientist in charge of the animal lab greets Laura, rubbing his hands together enthusiastically. "Doctor Solomon. How wonderful of you to stop by."

Forcing a smile, Laura fails to keep her eyes on her employee while they shake hands. She stares at another mouse she missed during her first sweeping appraisal of the lab. It's hiding behind a moss-covered rock in the snake's terrarium. Shaking, waiting, it watches the snake approach its pathetic hiding place.

"The simulations are improving tremendously, doctor." The man turns and walks to a screen that is taller than Laura. If she were to put on her AR-glasses, she'd see chemical formulas and numbers flickering across its surface. But she can't bring herself to focus. The snake now hovers on top of the rock, about to attack its breakfast from above.

"The substance is widely tested. All the mammal test subjects are doing well. Soon, we'll be able to integrate the nano technology with the virtual . . . "

"It's very promising, Mikko."

"It's Mika, actually."

Laura finally tears her gaze from the snake and stares at the man. "Is it really?"

A short, nervous laugh. "Last I checked, yes. My name is Mika, not Mikko."

"Hm. I could have sworn . . ."

Laura stares at the mouse. Soon, the snake would turn in under the rock and wrap into a bundle. There would be a lump under its skin, shaped like a mouse, mutating the snake's coiled form into something unnatural. *A snake eating a mouse is the most natural thing*, she reminds herself. *Why should it bother me?*

Mika clears his throat. "Doctor Solomon," he says. "If you don't mind me asking. Are you okay?"

Laura walks to the glass boxes, leaning closer to the snake. Its black and diamond-shaped head is now resting peacefully. And so is the mouse. Finally at rest. No more shaking in terror, no more waiting.

She sidesteps to another glass box, the one with the rabbit that once traveled with the rebels. "How is the rabbit doing, Mikko?"

"It's Mika," he says, looking more awkward by the minute. "The Oryctolagus cuniculus testing is just around the corner. Would you like to expedite the—"

"That won't be necessary," Laura says. She puts on the AR-glasses and taps open a control panel. She enters a password, taps in a pin code. The outer wall of the glass box slides open. Laura pushes the AR-glasses on top of her forehead and steps closer. The rabbit backs away into a corner, its small nose moving rapidly. Its wide black eyes are staring at her as though, instead of a white lab coat, she's suddenly wearing a zigzag pattern, her tongue split in two.

"At the back of its neck," Mika says. She didn't notice him approaching.

"What?"

The rabbit pushes against the back wall.

"They have loose skin at the back of their necks. People sometimes try to pick them up by their ears, but the cartilage can't hold the rabbit's weight. Lift from the neck, and it'll remain undamaged."

Laura turns and stares at the man in wonder. He lifts his hands and takes a step back.

"Unless that's not something you care about. I mean, you know best."

"Why wouldn't I care?"

The man's face flushes red. "I'm sorry?"

"Of course I don't want the rabbit to suffer. Why does everyone keep assuming otherwise?"

"I didn't . . . I don't . . . "

Laura turns and reaches for the bunny. Instead of reaching for the long ears or the back of its neck, she gently places her hands under its stomach area and lifts. The bunny relaxes against her grip.

"Ah, see. It's playing dead," Mika says. "Paralyzed by fear."

Laura holds the rabbit against her chest, patting its head. Long whiskers tickle the back of her palm. The short hair is like silk against her skin, as she strokes the critter and walks away.

"Don't worry. I know how to bring him back to life."

The helicopter takes off with Laura sitting next to the pilot. Instead of looking out the window, Laura focuses on reading the last board meeting memo through her AR-glasses. Not many people know about her fear of heights. The pilot starts talking to her, but Laura raises one hand to tell him to zip it. She wants to leave the helicopter behind, and with it the fear of crashing and burning. But the thought of entering a simulation without the comfort of her gaming chair makes her as dizzy as the distance between her and the Chip-Center's roof.

She'll need to remember to talk to Mikko about that once she returns from The United Inland. Taking a relaxing sedative pill would usually be inconceivable to her. But if Laura had any pills right now, she'd swallow a handful of them without a second thought.

There's also the option of mind remapping. In a matter of a few hours, Nurse Saarinen could erase her fear of heights, improving Laura's quality of life. Maybe she could finally visit the balcony of her penthouse and take in the view. But something holds her back. The fear is there for a reason, or so she believes.

Without it, would she be more prone to accidents? Would she even be herself anymore?

Shaking her head, Laura forces herself to focus on the memo in front of her eyes. The region she's traveling to—The United Inland—has changed a lot since the day Basile Keller was put in a stasis capsule far, far away. Over the years, as City of Serbia started to become stronger and more organized, Iris and her soldiers have been able to keep people in The United Inland in their designated cities, their designated jobs, and their somewhat controllable mental states. But the inquiries about future opportunities for travel, moving, or changing the way the Solomon Foundation runs the world keep coming in.

Then the news of the Iceland incident got out. Soon, Iris's reports started to include a lot fewer examples of troubled Inland citizens asking questions they shouldn't ask. They finally understood what others had figured out long ago: better keep it quiet. Because they wouldn't like the answers Iris had to give them anyway. Just as they wouldn't like their only option if they did move from their current location: a stasis capsule.

City of England's engineered plague should have been enough to kill people's urge to see beyond their designated city walls. Add the fact that something in the Iceland air had driven the Chipped rebels insane, turning them into cold-blooded killers. Laura shakes her head. How much more convincing would these simple minds need? Before they'd stop nagging about the things that used to be, and focus on the better life Laura's hard work has created for them?

Drained and exhausted, Laura dozes off. Dreaming of happily grinning Sanna, holding a rabbit with a snake's head, she keeps the AR-glasses on and lets the helicopter carry her further and further away from her comfort zone.

Standing in the middle of the stage, Laura breathes in the atmosphere. She scans the audience, counts in her head. *Thirty-five, forty, forty-five* . . . A much smaller crowd than she'd prefer. A familiar-looking head of hair stands out from the rows of people wearing AR-glasses. Blue and white locks frame Iris's unique face, making her look like something out of the storybooks Laura's started to read to Sanna and Mister Bun-Bun in the evenings. Most nights, it's not enough; the girl still asks for Markus after her own screams awaken her. Still, she's settled for Laura once or twice, and a story of a charmed fairy in a magical forest.

Laura gives Iris a smile. The Icelandic woman nods at her and taps her AR-glasses. When an envelope icon appears at the corner of Laura's vision, she taps it open and reads Iris's message.

WE NEED TO TALK. IT'S LEWIS. SHE CROSSED A LINE.

So it's not just Laura's head that Margaret is messing with.

Laura thinks of the words, then swipes to send.

MEET ME AT THE SPA AFTER.

Another nod. Iris crosses her arms on her chest, settling in her seat to wait for Laura's speech. The meetings have been like this ever since Laura's mother, Mrs. Salonen, resigned from her leading role. Along with three other founders that had stepped on Laura's toes one too many times. She should have stored Margaret in Iceland too—she can see that now. But Margaret had been too valuable with her god-like programming skills. Now, those skills are the invisible enemy keeping Laura awake at night—ever since the deaf woman hacked into her brain two weeks ago. At least the guard code Iris created seems to have done its job. Margaret hasn't visited Laura ever since Iris successfully updated the firewall in Laura's chipped brain.

As she raises her hand, the chattering comes to an end. People sit in their seats, focusing on their leader up on the stage. Laura takes her time, seeking eye contact with those at the back, those in the middle, and those sitting at the front. Chin high, she spreads her hands and smiles.

"Dear colleagues. Welcome."

The applause echoes from the conference room walls. Laura breathes it in, now standing inches taller, filling her lungs with the undeniable power that is her influence. She takes her time, enjoying the sight of people clapping their hands and nodding at her approvingly. Only those who agree with her, those who share her vision, are left. As it should have been from the beginning.

Folding her hands, Laura starts her slow walk around the front of the stage.

"First of all, I want to acknowledge the tremendous work you've done with nano technology. Together with our best programmers, my team has developed new procedures to bring a Chipped mind back after one of the unfortunate glitches that sometimes takes place in the system. Without your hard work, the Iceland incident could have been much deadlier than it turned out to be. So pat yourselves on the back. Not all heroes wear capes. Some of them wear lab coats and have dark circles under their eyes." Laura pauses briefly as they laugh. "So I want to say thank you. It was you who saved the day this time—not me."

The applause is fierce. She interrupts it faster this time, knowing very well that none of these intermediate scientists would have done shit if it wasn't for Nurse Saarinen and herself leading them from behind the scenes.

"Secondly, I would like to take a moment to talk about the progress we've made with mind mapping as well as memory and behavior remapping. As you all know, it has become imperative for us to restrict some of the more harmful human urges—"

"Is that. What you. Call it?"

Laura stumbles on her own feet but catches her balance just in time. *Not now*, she thinks. *Any other time. Just not now.*

Her audience stares at her in wonder. Nurse Saarinen clears her throat somewhere nearby. Startled, Laura takes a deep breath to continue her speech. She looks up and smiles. "Forgive me. It seems the helicopter has given me vertigo."

Smiles and approving nods encourage her to continue.

"As I was saying—"

"Tell them. About. Ava."

Mouth open, she stops to collect her thoughts. After shaking her head slightly, she continues to walk the stage. "The together with the ever-improving and updating implant—"

"You remember. Ava. Right? The girl. You murdered?"

This time she bends all the way over as if to escape Margaret's booming voice. Holding her head, Laura focuses on breathing and forces her body upright. *You won't beat me, Lewis*, she thinks, speaking to Margaret wordlessly inside her own mind. The experience makes her light-headed. It forces her to take off her AR-glasses so she can once again differentiate between the multiple realities she's experiencing.

A few of her colleagues are standing up now. Iris is one of them. The young woman frowns and takes a step closer to the stage. Iris knows what's going on. She's the only one in this room who does.

Laura stands tall, shaking her head slightly. A convincing smile painted on her face, she clears her throat and continues to speak to the crowd, "But you must be tired of hearing my voice by now. Why don't we hear from the mastermind behind the trials herself?" Margaret's voice still resonating between her ears, Laura turns and gestures toward Nurse Saarinen. "Dear colleagues, I give you Nurse Saarinen."

After the redhead walks onto the stage, Laura shakes Nurse Saarinen's hand.

"What the hell, Laura?" the nurse whispers.

Laura parts her dry lips to answer, but nothing comes out. Shaking her head, Laura turns her back on her audience and puts her AR-glasses on. Multiple envelope icons jump into her AR-mailbox. Too dizzy to open any of them, Laura storms out through the backstage, dropping the glasses into a metal trash can by the exit.

The sauna is not hot enough for her tastes. It rarely is outside of City of Finland. Silent and overwhelmed, Laura sits on the top bench, staring into the dim light that shines from under the sauna stove—*the kiuas*. She reaches for the ladle and the wooden bucket, throws more water on the hot rocks. Steam rises and fills the room. Laura sits back and closes her eyes.

She hears the sauna door open but doesn't bother to check who dares to disturb her privacy. The bench creaks slightly as someone sits opposite Laura.

"She's getting to you. Isn't she?"

Laura turns her face toward the sound. She opens her eyes to see Iris, wrapped in an oversized towel.

"What makes you say that?" Laura asks, smiling, her eyes barely open. "Maybe I'm just having a nervous breakdown."

Iris frowns and turns to look at the water bucket. She reaches for the wooden ladle but doesn't throw any water. Instead, she investigates the swirls and patterns in the wood. "Then we're in deeper trouble than I thought," she says. She leans forward and fills the ladle with water. When she tosses the water on the *kiuas*, only a portion of it lands on the rocks. The hissing sound makes Laura close her eyes again.

They sit in silence for a good while, Laura drifting from wakefulness to sleep. At some point, Iris moves down on the benches but keeps throwing water to keep the temperature up. She knows Laura likes her saunas hot. In some ways, the young woman knows more about her than Nurse Saarinen does. How that's possible, Laura doesn't know. Iris isn't a fan of asking questions.

"The guard code failed," Iris finally says, snapping Laura back into this moment and time.

"It did."

Overwhelming fatigue pushes Laura's shoulders down. Her eyelids feel heavy, and her tongue is almost numb in her mouth. Falling asleep in a hot sauna isn't a good idea, but Laura fails to care.

As if she's reading Laura's mind, Iris hands her a plastic water bottle. "Margaret's work is way ahead of ours. It's one thing to turn off someone's chip or enter a command code like we did in Iceland. But being able to access a mind like that. To come and go as she pleases . . ."

Laura twists the bottle cap open and takes a long gulp. "It's bullshit. That's what it is." Water dribbles out of her mouth and onto her chin. From there, it trails down her naked body. Laura appreciates Iris not answering right away. She enjoys the sensation of fresh water entering her dehydrated body.

"I can fix that."

"I know you can, dear."

Iris turns to look at Laura. Unlike most of Laura's colleagues, the girl has no problem staring at her, buck naked or not. Iris has never been intimidated by such things. Her focus seems on point, no matter what her job as the Head Programmer of the Happiness-Program throws her way.

"I just need a day. Maybe two."

Laura smiles but doesn't answer. She lifts her feet and places them up against the wooden railing, then closes her eyes.

Just as she's about to doze off again, the bench underneath her creaks. Iris climbs down to leave the sauna, turns around and hands Laura the wooden ladle. She stares at her awhile, clearly wanting to say something. Then she shakes her head instead, blue and white locks dancing around her fairy face. She walks out without a word.

What used to be the streets of Paris open in front of Laura. It being nighttime, and her having tossed her AR-glasses in the conference center's trash can, makes the world seem brand new. This part of the Inlands barely has any AR-technology. City of Serbia is the closest fully operating AR-city. Most of the places in what used to be Europe—regions like France, Germany, Hungary, and Spain—now function as storage and meeting spaces for those in charge.

A spa robe wrapped around her, Laura walks down the street. The full moon illuminates her path. She can't remember the last time she saw this many stars in the sky. Any stars. The light pollution is usually everywhere, at least back home. The silence around her makes her ears ring, and the ground under her slippers seems harder than usual. More real. Somehow more convincing.

Random thoughts take over. Against her usual habits, she lets them.

Had her daughter walked here once? Visited The United Inland? Laura knows no details about her travels with the Unchipped. Did Sanna ever stroll down this same damaged road?

It's unlikely. Kaarina, the lowlife behind this short and useless rebellion, had kept those who followed her far away from civilization. Margaret helping them, the rebels had always been one step ahead of Laura and her team, the deaf woman guiding them away from locations filled with Chipped leaders.

Not anymore.

All the Unchipped rebels now rest in their designated stasis capsules, shipped back to the cities where they belong. There, they'll sleep until Laura finds a way to convert their malfunctioning brains for good. But she'll need to succeed with the Chipped first. If she can't keep people like Markus in the city willingly, how can she to control a subject like Kaarina or the mountain of a man she traveled with?

The street turns into an alleyway. Laura walks on in the warm night, looking at partly unhinged signs above what used to be boutiques and boulangeries, selling fresh French loaves and coffee with a shot of liquor mixed in. She walks into the darkness, completely alone and away from the reality she has full control over. She stops under a sign that says something in French. This part of The United Inland was the only region that never adapted to speaking English. The people refused to give up on their native ways and traditions. That's one of the biggest reasons why City of France was never built: The people here were too stubborn to be controlled.

Laura looks up at the sky. Margaret's voice seems to have left her head in a congested state she's never experienced before. Like she's out of place, unrooted. Or is it Sanna? Those big innocent eyes of hers, staring into Laura's soul like a trapped mind inside a creepy porcelain doll?

The sound of her own scream pierces the air. It hurts her ears but feels good. Better than the weight of AR-glasses against her face. Or an audience standing and applauding. A controlled pack. Empty of thoughts and wants, but filled with value and a fruitful future.

She screams again.

And again.

When she lies down on the cold concrete and lets the exhaustion take her over, Laura imagines hearing another heartbeat pounding against the back of her skull.

"I just don't get why you'd take off like that."

Ducking their heads, Nurse Saarinen and Laura speed walk away from the helicopter and toward the rooftop doorway of City of Finland's Chip-Center. The stiffness in Laura's neck and the nagging nerve pain in her right shoulder remind her of a night spent under the stars. It was Iris who had found her, out cold in the middle of a dark alleyway. But not even Iris was smart enough to come up with a lie that Nurse Saarinen would believe. And ever since learning about Laura's nighttime adventure, Nurse Saarinen has been in a terrible mood.

"Who knows who's out there," she had mumbled, turning her back on Iris and Laura. To update Laura's chip guard codes, Iris had traveled with them to City of Finland. This had also irritated Nurse Saarinen.

"Don't you think you should return to City of Serbia?" she had said to Iris. "Especially now that this deaf lunatic is roaming around who knows where."

"Margaret won't be a problem," Iris had said. "And don't you worry about my city. I've got it covered."

"You mean Jovan's got it covered? Tell me again, how does a maintenance man slash soldier end up in charge of the IT department?"

"He's none of your concern."

"Ah, really? Last I checked, you weren't the COO around here—"

"Okay, hey." Laura had raised her hand. "Give it a rest, will you? I'm fine, and if Iris says Jovan can be in charge while she's gone, I trust her judgment. As for last night, I just needed some fresh air, got dehydrated after my sauna, and needed to gather my strength before heading back to the hotel. I guess I lost track of time."

Neither of the women had looked convinced, but they fell silent anyway. Now they're heading down the stairs, clearly eager to get rid of one another.

Laura sighs and presses the elevator button. "Iris, give me five, and I'll meet you down there. I just need to check up on something."

Iris nods and heads to the staircase, carrying a hefty duffel bag over her shoulder.

"You don't need a lift?" Laura hollers after her.

"I'm good!" Iris yells back, disappearing into the fire stairwell.

Nurse Saarinen walks into the elevator and presses the penthouse button. As the lift starts moving, she taps her foot against the floor and stares straight ahead.

"Owena's moved in with the new family."

"I see," Laura says. "Too bad the first one wasn't a match."

"The second one wasn't, either. This is our third try."

She stops and frowns. "Really? So none of the code adoptions are working?"

"Doesn't seem so, no. Just the pills. The research would be much faster if we had two children—"

"The pills should be enough to keep a small girl under control," Laura says, interrupting Nurse Saarinen before she can elaborate on her plans for Sanna. The girl's still not scheduled for chipping, and it seems to bother Nurse Saarinen more than anything else. The fact that the girl is Unchipped and therefore at much greater risk of failing any operation seems to have completely slipped Nurse Saarinen's mind. Or maybe she doesn't care. She's right, though. To figure out the chip repair, they do need more Unchipped individuals to test with.

"Why are the families giving up on Owena so quickly?" Laura asks, hoping to distract Nurse Saarinen enough that she'll forget about Sanna for the time being.

The doors slide open, and Laura walks out. She blocks the elevator door from closing and waits to hear Nurse Saarinen's explanation.

"She's more violent than we thought. Owena."

"But we knew this. That's why we chose her. Are you choosing couples with high social ranks?" Laura waits for a nod. "Then they should be able to deal with a couple of temper tantrums."

"She attacked her foster mother while the woman was asleep. Gave her two black eyes and a nosebleed."

"Bloody hell."

"Mm."

"Should we put her back under?"

Nurse Saarinen shrugs and presses the button below the penthouse icon. Her apartment is one floor below Laura's and Sanna's. "Could send the wrong message. She's not Chipless anymore, she's part of the program. People would start talking about her."

"Why would people talk about Owena?"

"They know she grew up in Kinship Care. She survived the plague and killed a woman. Then traveled with the rebels and survived the Iceland incident. Little shit's quite famous around here."

Laura frowns. "People still gossip like that? I thought we were monitoring gossip and rebellious conversations."

"We are."

"Then what happened to trigger words and mutineer alerts?"

Nurse Saarinen gestures for Laura to move her hand. But she keeps it where it is, blocking the elevator from leaving.

"They've been talking at work. Before plugging in and pedaling. We might have the rebels contained, but there are still some aftereffects that need to be taken care of. Which reminds me…" Nurse Saarinen nods at Laura's hand again. "We'd better get to work."

"And then Markus lifted Mister Bun-Bun onto his shoulder and called him a pirate!"

Sanna's eyes beam with excitement as she tells the story to Laura. The girl sits in the middle of the floor, surrounded by puzzle pieces. It's getting harder and harder to find things to keep her occupied. But without a working chip in her brain, the girl can only visit the city for fifteen or twenty minutes at a time. A larger one-time dose of blockers could do some serious damage to her brain. Laura's asked Nurse Saarinen to run more tests on the blockers, but she waves her hand each time. "Those things?" she'd say. "Why bother? Soon we won't need them at all. Not with zero Unchipped around."

Laura has tried to talk about the chipping operation with Sanna. She's brought up the fact that the child is different. She's asked if she'd like to be like everyone else, to watch cool AR-movies and play games with others her age. Stay in the city for longer than a quick U-turn. Go to school.

"Sanna, sweetie," Laura starts her mantra once again, careful not to push too hard. The chipping needs to be the girl's own idea. Why it's so important to Laura, she's not sure. But the thought of forcing Sanna through the operation feels more and more revolting every time Laura is with her. "Have you thought about what we talked about before my trip?"

Sanna's down on all fours, hovering over the puzzle, trying to find the next missing piece. "About making friends?" she asks.

"Yes." Laura steps closer to the girl, then stops to lean on the wall under the teddy bear and porcelain doll. "Wouldn't it be nice to have someone to play with?"

A shrug. Then an excited look when she finds a potential missing piece. Locks of black hair hanging over her face, Sanna tries to fit the piece in, then tosses it back on top of the pile. "But I already have a friend. Markus. I like Markus."

Laura sighs and folds her hands behind her back. "But what about kids your own age?"

"What about them?"

"Wouldn't you like to do what they're doing?"

"I don't know," Sanna says. She stops to ponder Laura's words. "What are they doing?"

"A number of things, sweetie. They visit the AR-zoo. Have ice cream in the city. Watch the newest AR-shows. There's even a simulation where you can meet up with multiple friends at once. Together, you could build a puzzle ten times that big. And you can decide what kind of a puzzle it is, choose any picture you want. Cool colors and even music."

"A puzzle with music?" Sanna pouts, staring into the pile of misfit pieces. "Doesn't sound like a real puzzle to me." She picks a new piece, trying to finish a white cloud above a rapeseed field. "Markus is really good with puzzles. Bill was too. Kaarina and Luna were always too busy working, but I'm sure they would help me if I asked them to. Can Markus bring them with him tonight? I would love to see them all. I miss them. Especially Micky."

Fists closing, Laura takes a deep breath. This is not working. The girl's too young to understand what's good for her. How she needs to be normal and start living her new life.

"Sweetie, sooner or later, you'll need to become a part of this city. You have to forget about Markus and all those people you were stuck with."

"But why?"

"Because they're bad people, Sanna. They took you away from . . . " Laura clears her throat. "They took you away from your home and refused to let us come rescue you. You could have ended up hurt or worse."

"What do you mean worse?" Eyes wide and filled with horror, Sanna looks up at Laura. "Could I have ended up like a robot? Like that day when Niina's eyes changed color, and she stopped talking?"

This conversation has gotten out of hand, but Laura doesn't know how to fix it. She has zero experience when it comes to talking to children. "Niina protected you. I made her."

"How? And why did you make her eyes glow like that?" Sanna closes the puzzle piece into her small fist. "She looked really scary. I wish you hadn't done that."

It's frustrating, having no idea how to explain any of this to a kid. *Well, sweetie,* she plays with the thought of just laying it all on her. *While researching the override protocol, I noticed how the gene expression that followed this particular chip update caused a phosphorescence in the cerebrospinal fluid, and the aqueous humor that fills the anterior chamber of the eye . . .*

"She looked kind of like you do right now," Sanna says, interrupting Laura's deep thoughts. "Like she was somewhere else."

"It doesn't really matter, sweetie. All you need to know is that I did it all for you. Niina kept you and Owena safe while . . . "

While the other Chipped took care of the fuckers that took away my daughter.

"While I put a stop to what Kaarina and the others were doing."

"That doesn't make any sense. They weren't doing anything bad. They told us really good stories at the pool. And baked us *pulla.* And let us pet the horses and feed them peppermints. You're not making any sense, Doctor Solomon."

"Please, sweetie. Call me Laura."

"Why did her eyes glow, Laura?"

"Because of the chip in her brain. We had to program Niina's code so that she wouldn't let anything bad happen to you."

"The chip does that?" Sanna gasps, and her eyes grow even wider. "Gives you robot eyes?"

"No, not usually. The chip is a good thing. It helps you live a better life. Makes you feel good."

"Like I do when I'm with Mister Bun-Bun and Markus?"

Knuckles white, Laura counts in her head. *Five, six, seven, eight.*

"The chip will let you play with children your own age. It'll let you fit in."

"Fit in where?"

"In the city."

"But I'm back in the city already."

"You're in the Chip-Center. The city is where we go for walks. Until you feel too sick to continue."

Sanna thinks for a few seconds. Then her face clears. "Ah, yes. Where the invisible animals live."

Laura smiles and exhales. "Exactly. Wouldn't it be nice to live there? With the butterflies and rabbits?"

Sanna shakes her head. "No. I don't like it there."

"But you just said…" Laura knows she should leave the room. Try again later when she's better rested. "Why don't you like it there?"

"Because it makes my tummy and head hurt."

"But it wouldn't. Not if you had the chip."

"But then I'd have robot eyes."

"No, you wouldn't." Laura's voice is too stern. She's about to lose her temper.

Six, seven, eight, nine, ten.

"Sweetie. If you get the chip, you would be just like everyone else. You'd be normal."

Sanna leans forward to hover over the puzzle. She tries on another piece, and this time it sinks into its slot effortlessly. She smiles and looks up. "Kaarina always said it's okay to be different. That normal is boring."

"Oh, for fuck's sake!"

Laura's forceful words echo in the room, and for a moment, they both stare at each other. Then Sanna's eyes water. She stands up and backs over to her bed, dives under the sheets.

Shit, shit, shit.

"Sweetie, I didn't mean to yell at you."

A muffled sob. The girl presses against the wall, hiding under the blanket.

"Sanna, please. I'm sorry. It's more complicated than that. You'll get it all once you're a bit older. People need help, and that's what the city is for. It cures them of bad things—"

A louder sob. She shouldn't have brought up 'bad things.'

Chin tucked, Laura fingers the AR-glasses in her pocket. Iris has been waiting in the lab for at least thirty minutes. Laura's terribly late. Margaret could have made a move against her at any moment while she's been having this mindless and useless conversation.

"I'm sorry, sweetie. We can talk some other time. I'm sorry I yelled."

More sobs.

"Can I get you anything? Before I go?"

The sobbing ends. Eyes mixed with fear and hopefulness peek from under the blanket.

"Yes."

"And what's that, sweetie?"

"Can Markus come over early?"

The chipping helmet tight around her head, Laura tries to make herself comfortable in the stasis capsule. The door is open, and Nurse Saarinen hovers nearby, watching Iris's every move. The young woman has been staring into the screens for over an hour, switching from one CS-key to another. Every now and then she mumbles something in her native language, comes over and checks the helmet wiring, then sits in front of the screens again.

Nurse Saarinen taps the capsule's glass door with her knuckles. "Are you sure you wouldn't prefer the operation table?"

"I'm fine. Stop hovering."

With a lower voice, Nurse Saarinen says, "I don't trust the kid." She's now leaning into the capsule, her high forehead only a few inches from Laura.

"Well, I do. Iris is one of our best. Why don't you go check the test subject simulation results? While we do this?" Laura shrugs against the soft capsule walls. "Who knows, maybe we can keep this one awake for more testing?"

"Doubt it," Nurse Saarinen says, but turns to leave anyway. "I'm starting to think the Unchipped are some sort of mutation."

"Mutations, huh?"

Laura's amused question makes Iris peek up from the screens. Her gaze flickers between Laura and Nurse Saarinen.

"Yeah. Creatures from another world," Nurse Saarinen continues. "Uncontrollable pests. That sort of thing."

"And what if they are?" Iris asks, no trace of amusement in her voice.

Nurse Saarinen shrugs and turns to leave. "You know. Kill it with fire."

Iris stares after her for a while, then she snaps her attention back to the task at hand. With a serious face, she picks up one of the CS-keys and walks over to Laura. "I've updated the code and added a firewall ten times stronger than the one we were using before."

"I see."

"How are you feeling?"

"Dizzy. Blurry. Dreamy."

"Good."

Laura laughs briefly. "How is any of that good, dear?"

"It tells us your brain is already adjusting to the changes. Without delay."

A prickling sensation travels across Laura's skull. She swallows and focuses on keeping her face blank of expression. If she showed the level of discomfort she's actually in, there's no way Iris would let her get back to work after the update is done.

"What else could you do? If I asked you to?"

Iris cocks her head at Laura's question, the CS-key at eye level. Finally, she fixes her gaze on Laura's. "What do you mean, what else? Another update? You want better sleep? Appetite? What?"

"No, no. Not for me." Laura thinks for a while, hesitating. "Say I was someone else. Someone recently upgraded. Just an ordinary Chipped person about to be integrated with the CS and the city."

"Okay. And?"

"And I would need a bit . . . *extra* to feel good."

Iris frowns and sets the CS-key back on the table. She stares straight at Laura, trying to read her face to understand the meaning behind these random questions. "I'm sorry. *Extra*?"

"Say I was younger and badly damaged by the people I grew up with. I have trust issues, and I'm terribly confused about everything."

"Everything?"

"Yes, life in general."

"Like what to eat and where to sleep?"

"Like who to listen to. Who I can trust. And, well . . . love."

Iris stays quiet for a while. She sucks in her lower lip, pondering what to say next.

"You're asking me if I could make you love someone? Like we made Niina protect Sanna and Owena in Iceland?"

Laura doesn't say anything. With a blank look on her face, she keeps staring back at Iris. Finally, the girl drops her stare.

"Well, I mean. We could use the coding we've created for Fertility Treatment. But that project is years away from its first injection. I mean, you know what happened to Niina after Iceland."

"Yes. She died."

Iris's lips parted, she stares at Laura. "That's right. We literally fried her brain." Iris searches Laura's face for emotion. Regret. Laura can tell. But her face remains neutral.

"Okay . . . " Iris turns away and returns to sit by the screens. "What are you suggesting here? Should

I proceed with the mind control coding to solve the Iceland-bug?"

"You should."

"And what about Margaret?"

"What about her?"

"She's a step ahead of us again. Multiple steps. I mean, she hacked into Chipped brains. And not just any brains, yours and mine. Her code is well beyond and further along than what—"

"What did she tell you?"

Iris frowns, again staring at Laura. "What? Who?"

"Margaret. When she hacked your chip and talked to you. What did she say?"

Iris fixes her weight on the lab stool she's sitting on. Dodging Laura's searching eyes, she focuses on plucking invisible lint off her lab coat.

"Well?"

"Does it matter what she said? Lewis is a lunatic. She's too far off in her own reality to see what we're trying to achieve here. Her dreams of a free world were more childish and pathetic than useful. Too bad, though. We could use her programming skills. They're out of this world, just like her mind."

"What did she say to you?"

Iris bites her lower lip. Then she sighs, shrugging a shoulder. "She said I could go home. If I wanted to."

Iris wipes her hands on her pants. "She said I could start all over."

"In Iceland?"

A nod. "Yeah. At the resort."

"Live alone in the middle of nothingness?"

A shrug. "Like I said, the woman is insane."

"And you can't tell where she's located? Not even if it's West-Land or East-Land?"

"Not for sure, no. But I do have a guess."

Laura scoffs and smiles. "Well, dear. I'm all ears. Spit it out."

Iris shrugs a shoulder. "I didn't say it's something I can prove. It's more like an educated guess. Just something she said before I got her out of my head."

"About you going back home?"

"Before that. Something about being surrounded by mountains and silverpuffs. How she can understand why I would miss it so much."

"What the hell are silverpuffs?"

"They're flowers. Margaret must think they grow in Iceland, but they don't. Or maybe she was just looking around, describing the scenery. And as far as I know, the only place where silverpuffs grow is—"

"California."

A *bling* sound from one of the screens makes Iris turn her back and refocus. "Okay, this might make your ears ring a bit," she says. "Tell me if you become nauseated, and I'll bring you a brown bag."

Laura closes her eyes, doing her best to ignore the sensation of a hundred ants gnawing their way through her skull and into her brain. She is nauseated, but her stomach started feeling that way before Iris attached the chipping helmet to her head. It started a long time ago. Last year, when she walked into Sanna's room in the Chip-Center, only to notice the window wide open and the girl gone. Kidnapped. It shouldn't have made her sick to her stomach—losing her daughter. Because before that moment, she had hardly cared. Sanna was test subject number one. Her own flesh and bones. From the time before she became the ruler of a collapsed world.

CHAPTER 3
10 YEARS EARLIER

Helsinki, Finland, 2079

A recording of birds singing plays through the bathroom speakers. Everyone in the meeting room is waiting for her to hurry back. At least that's what Laura has asked them to do before going ahead with the agenda. It's not her fault she needs to pee every ten minutes. It's the fucking baby—pressing against her bladder.

The toilet paper roll in her hands, Laura reads the booth wall. No one at Pharma Salonen is young enough to doodle on a bathroom wall. Or so she had thought.

"Ignorant assbrains . . ." she mumbles, wrapping the soft tissue around her hand. Laura leans closer to the booth wall. With one finger, she traces the doodle on the white surface. She's surprised her mother hasn't had the walls painted orange, or red, or yellow, like every wall in the house Laura grew up in. "I don't like white walls," Mrs. Salonen used to tell her when she was only knee high. "It makes me feel like I'm living inside an egg."

Scratching the pencil mark off the toilet booth, Laura watches as the critter's head disappears in front of her eyes. A beaver? Maybe a squirrel.

"Disrespectful low-lifes . . . "

As she gets up, the toilet flushes automatically. Once the booth door opens, a faucet starts running in the sink. She needs to place her enormous belly on top of the sink to wash her hands. The human growing inside her can pop out any day as far as she's concerned. This was a bad idea. But it's too late to take it back now. What's done is done.

After washing her hands, Laura investigates her face in the mirror. A ripple of conversation reaches her ears through the vent, telling her that the great Mrs. Salonen has treated the team to an extra five-minute break.

In the mirror, Laura's eyes look sharp, the tops of her cheeks flushed. If she was just a regular pregnant woman, she'd tell herself that she's glowing. Happiness, sparkling through her pores and shiny eyes. "When's the due date?" they'd all ask. And she would pat her stupid belly and smile and joke. "Not a day too soon." She'd let people help her sit down on a hefty armchair. Let them bring her chamomile water and aloe lotion. "And which is it? A boy or a girl?"

The questions wouldn't irritate her if she was like all the other moms out there. Thoughts like "What's it to you?" and "Go sniff someone else's uterus, you nosey fuck-face" would never flash through her mind like they do today. No. If she was an ordinary pregnant woman, she'd say, "Oh, we don't care if it's a boy or a girl. A healthy baby. That's all we wish for."

But there's no "we." No use for wishful thinking or curiosity. It's a girl. It will have the black hair and brown eyes of its donor father. Not that Laura really cares about colors. Living inside an egg wouldn't bother her one bit.

She leans close to the mirror, staring into green eyes filled with ambition and above-average intelligence. "What a load of shit . . . " she mumbles.

Because that's what they are—the ordinary women and men and children. Average. Useless. Valueless, with their little catchphrases and their idiotic hopes and dreams. While one of them gives birth to another mediocre human being, a thousand others step off a chair with a noose tied around their necks. Or that's what the diligent cowards do. The lazy ones lie to their shrinks and doctors to score an extra bottle of Benzodoxepidem.

The baby kicks against the white sink. Before Laura can stop herself, her hands hurry to hug her stomach. Even she can't fight all her maternal instincts. But she can fight for this world. Fix humanity. Become the one who should have been in charge all along.

Basile Keller leans back in his chair, his suit sharp and his skin perfect, making him look like a model from the AR-catalog. The French man is listening to Mrs. Salonen, shaking his head every now and then, writing notes in a yellow-paged notebook. Despite his arrogant ways and his complete inability—or unwillingness—to read a room, Laura's always tolerated him a bit better than the rest. The man is annoying, but at least they think alike. And when Laura's mother continues to empathize with what she calls "the victims of the addiction crisis," Basile and Laura scoff at the same time. He looks at Laura, raising his eyebrows. Laura gestures for him to go ahead.

Basile sits tall in his chair and pushes his notes across the table. "See, Mrs. Salonen. Here's where you're wrong. These people, your so-called victims, have been given several chances to become upstanding citizens and prove their worth. Being soft and understanding is only letting them take advantage of our society's already insufficient resources. None of us can deny that to criminalize and eliminate is— what—ten times more cost efficient?"

Laura presses her lips together to hide her smile. *Mother's not going to like that*, she thinks. Tilting her head, she studies Mrs. Salonen's reaction. Listens to her words. How she mirrors Basile's posture, placing her hands on the table the exact same way. How she repeats his words. "If I hear you right, you're saying..." *Blah blah blah*. "Is that correct, dear?"

Why does she have to call everyone "dear?"

The conversation continues, but the words lose their meaning. It doesn't matter, Laura's heard this debate before. She's lost count of the number of times she's had this conversation with her mother. Instead of listening to their argument, Laura wants to learn how she does it, The Great Mrs. Salonen. Lead a group of scientists. Talk so that everyone listens. Whether people agree with her or not, no one ever interrupts her or talks over her. Respect. That's what Laura sees on every face around the conference table. Laura is endlessly fascinated by her own mother. The woman she's known for over thirty years. Her employer for ten of those years.

A gentle smile.

A friendly, but not pushy, touch.

Repeated words.

"I hear you, dear."

Memorizing each movement, each facial expression and phrase, Laura studies Mrs. Salonen closely. Not to become her, but to gain the power she has.

"So when's the big day?"

Basile has given someone else a turn to speak. His half-whispered question forces Laura to stop monitoring her mother.

"Excuse me?"

"The kid. When does baby Salonen see daylight?"

Laura shrugs her shoulders, then returns to staring at her mother. She wants to tell Basile to mind his own business. To shove his nosey questions where the sun doesn't shine. A wave of laughter fills the room. Mrs. Salonen has said something to lighten the mood. In the middle of a discussion about the world coming to an end.

Laura turns to smile at Basile. "It's not going to be 'Salonen.' The baby."

"Oh? I wasn't aware. Named after the father then?"

Laura studies his face. Tanned, some gray on his three-day beard. The man hasn't lost any hair, despite being in his early fifties.

"Solomon," she says. The donor form flashes through her mind, the one she had picked from hundreds of options. A scientist, of course. Why would she have chosen anything else? With a high IQ score. The highest she could find in the Fertility Center of Helsinki. All she lacked was the name. Only his initials were marked down: S.O.L.

"Why is this donor overlooked?" she had asked the nurse at the fertility center. "Is there something wrong with the viability of his sperm cells?"

But the nurse shook her head. "No, Miss Salonen—"

"Doctor Salonen."

"My apologies." The nurse had given her a quick smile. "Nothing wrong with the cells."

"What then?"

She had tapped the form in front of Laura, pointing out the initials. "They believe it's bad luck."

"Who does?"

"The patients. Our customers."

Laura had stared at the form in front of her, momentarily jumbled. "What? S.O.L.?"

A shrug. "Nobody wants to risk it. Not when it comes to this. It's too important."

Laura had scoffed. "Are people really *that* superstitious?"

Instead of a shrug, the nurse had given Laura a motherly look. "They say that all they know is that there is more than they know. None of us is above fate."

"Poor bastard just has unfortunate initials."

"It's bad luck."

"Shitty luck, you mean?"

"Excuse me? And there's no need for that kind of a language, Miss Salonen."

"Doctor."

Lips pressed into a thin line, the nurse had left the room, leaving Laura to fill out the rest of the paperwork.

Rolling her eyes, Laura snaps out of her memories. Basile is waving his hand in front of her blank stare.

"So you went shopping abroad then," he continues his mindless blabbering, a smile plastered on his well-aged face. For a moment, Laura wishes she could punch the guy. But to stop her mother and her ludicrous plan, she'll need an ally. Better play it nice.

"Yes . . . dear. Solomon like the father. He's from your neck of the woods, actually."

Lies.

"Ah, a French gentleman then? Good for you!"

This conversation is making Laura feel like a piece of plastic, a toy, or a Styrofoam lunch box. Disposable after use. How do other women do this? For the first time ever, for a split second, Laura understands why women tend to gather in flocks and leave the roosters out. This is her body, her private life. Why is it okay for anyone to ask her such personal questions, just because she's pregnant? Basile is hardly the first one to pry this information out of her. Information that Laura hasn't shared with anyone. Not even her own mother.

"Are you breastfeeding, then?"

Just as Laura opens her mouth to give Basile a piece of her mind, Mrs. Salonen calls her name. "Laura, sweetie." Her face flushes with frustration and anger. Now this. She's asked her mother not to call her that in public. Or anywhere else for that matter, but especially not at work.

"Yes, Mrs. Salonen?"

"You had some interesting development ideas when it comes to fertility rates and family affairs. Care to share those thoughts with us?"

Of course. Babies. That's all they think about when they look at her.

"Actually, I was wondering if we could talk about the healing aspect of the chip technology. How we should focus on behavior modification rather than healing diseases and disabilities. The helmet together with the nano—"

"This is not on the agenda today." It's Timofei Grisin who interrupts her. "The healing devices and mind mapping were discussed earlier this week—"

"Yes, they were," Laura says. "But every time I tried to add something, *somebody* would interrupt me in the middle of my sentence."

"Maybe people wouldn't do that if you stuck to the agenda."

"Maybe you could shove that agenda up your—"

"Okay! Okay." Mrs. Salonen stands up, gesturing for a truce. "Timofei, dear. I understand you're concerned about our limited time. But let's hear Laura out and then move on with the agenda. Is that okay with you?"

"I suppose," the man says. He folds his arms and leans back in his chair.

"Good. Laura. You were saying that the healing devices could use an upgrade? Did I understand that right, sweetie?"

"Not an upgrade. But an adaptation."

"I'm not sure I follow," Basile says, turning in his seat to get a better look at Laura. "How can there be more than one way to heal a damaged liver or a broken bone?"

"There isn't. I don't want to sew their bodies together, Basile. I want to alter their minds."

Timofei laughs briefly. A few others follow his lead, shaking their heads. Mrs. Salonen smiles and keeps her eyes on Laura.

"Okay. Interesting. And what would this mind-altering mean in practice?"

Laura stands up, doing her best not to bump into the table with her belly. She straightens her white blouse and looks around the table, dodging every curious gaze. How does her mother do this every single day? How does she do it with such ease?

"Well, to save time and stay on the agenda," she gives Timofei a dirty look, "let's use an example that also has to do with the drastically dropping fertility rates. Children. I think many, if not all of you, can agree that people can't be trusted with parenting anymore. Those who are not hospitalized because of mental issues, or dumping their kids on the streets because of sudden unemployment and lack of food, are seemingly okay parents who still raise offspring that, in four out of five cases, are reported to suffer from depression, anxiety, social disorders, or panic attacks. Our youth centers have been full for years, and even now, with the new phenomenon of mass-deaths, there's still a one-year waitlist for these individuals to get treatment and a safe place to live."

The more she talks, the better Laura feels about her own voice. She thinks of her mother, the things she monitored her doing earlier, and mirrors the way she moves, acts, and talks.

"Getting people to reproduce is not the answer here. Not if all they do is create more burdens for our social and health systems. We are being crushed under the weight of invalid, helpless children, teens, and young adults."

"But it's hardly. Their fault. Is it?"

Margaret Lewis. The woman has a rare disease that is slowly killing her hair follicles and rendering her deaf. As Margaret is known to avoid speaking out loud, it's uncommon for her to voice her concerns.

"Does it really matter, Margaret? Whose fault it is? What matters is that it's happening. While these overwhelmed, overworked, burned-out adults beg their governments for another pill, their children don't stand a chance. Not to be blunt, but I think in most cases their social-media-ruined parents offing themselves might be the best chance they have to live a somewhat normal life." Laura pauses for the ripple of gasps and murmurs, but only for a few seconds. "Why not let them contribute to society? Let them integrate with the system."

"Where would they grow up instead? In children's homes?" Mrs. Salonen asks, leaning her chin on her hands. She's sitting down again, listening to Laura carefully.

"Homes, boarding schools, the army. But above all, the nurseries. We already have children who grow up without parents, in the nursery and later on at a children's home. The data shows that these kids show a superior level of decency when it comes to adapting to the education system and later on building a career and a stable personal life. Leadership among these children is higher than with any other social class."

"So we just go around and kidnap everyone's kids? Is that your solution?" Timofei spreads his hands, looking at those around the table. He huffs loudly. "Give me a break."

"We don't kidnap them," Laura says, walking slowly and stopping behind Timofei's seat. The man doesn't turn to look at her. Laura can feel his irritation radiating from his thick skull. "We alter them. Fix the behavioral issues before they really begin."

"And the. Parents?"

"Give them the vodka-pill. Hell, give them whiskey and Ambien while you're at it. Let the weak weed themselves out. And those who truly want to become something valuable to this society—we alter them as well."

"And then what?" Basile asks. "Upload these improved individuals into the cloud?"

"Mind upload has nothing to do with this. But yes, Basile. Now that you brought it up, I do believe we should grant immortality to those who contribute to this world instead of destroying it. And it is therefore imperative that we prioritize our whole-brain emulation trials going forward."

When the gasps and objections continue, Mrs. Salonen stands and holds her hands up, demanding silence. Then she steps over to Laura, still standing behind the Russian scientist's back. "Sweetie. You have an excellent foundation here for something we can surely use. We just need to soften the approach a bit, don't you think? The parents you talked about? They are suffering as well, just in a different way than their children. These are all real people with real problems. Real, breathing, living beings. They all have worth, and they're all valuable in their own way. Even if we can't always see or understand what that way might be."

"Some have more value than others," Laura says. "Some build, create, and improve. While the others destroy, sabotage, and deteriorate."

"But the families—"

"The families?" Laura scoffs, amused.

A mass sterilization, that's all these so-called families have coming for them, as far as Laura's concerned. Little something-something added to their drinking water, and these peasant parents will never hurt another child with their incapable ways, ever again. Of course Laura can't share this plan, not with her mother in the room, anyway.

"Mother, have you read the news lately? Because I have. Guess what the headlines are, day after day, night after night? Domestic violence: *SARS-fearing father strangles teenage daughter for not washing her hands properly.* Mental issues: *Social-media addict and mother of three runs a whorehouse. Gets shut down by the police, leaving her two teen sons and a fifteen-year-old daughter unemployed.* Vending machines for sleeping pills and antidepressants to ease a hospital staff's workload. Another suicide committed by a social-media-bullied ten-year-old. And a twelve-year-old. And a twenty-one—"

Timofei grunts but doesn't turn around to face Laura and her mother. "We get it, Salonen."

"It's Solomon," Laura says, hissing between her teeth.

Her mother's head nudges back in surprise. "Solomon?"

"Yes. I've decided to change my name. And I suggest we change the plan for the chipping procedure and the stasis capsule as well. To something more practical than curing tumors in people who will only celebrate by mixing a cocktail of bleach and gin. We don't need to cure diabetes, we need to cure stupid. I mean, what else can you call a species that destroys itself the way ours has?"

Mrs. Salonen opens her mouth to reply, but her words fail her. Laura sidesteps away from her and heads for the conference room door. When she turns around to have the last word, she focuses on keeping her voice and her expression calm.

"And as for all of you asking questions about my uterus. You know, or about the sex of the person growing inside *my* body. Or about the man who allegedly stuffed his penis inside me to ensure there'd be at least one more citizen in this god-forsaken city with an IQ higher than seventy. To prove my point, and for this being's own good, this child is not going to grow up knowing his or her mother. Or father. Or any insignificant and useless information like that."

"Sweetie, you're clearly upset. Let's step outside—"

Laura waves off her mother. Waves off Basile, Margaret, and that fuck-turd that never lets her finish a sentence. But that time has come to its end. From now on, no one will step on Laura's toes or muffle her voice.

"This child will be born and raised in the nursery. Then altered through chipping. Becoming someone who truly deserves to live."

CHAPTER 4
UP HIGH

The gaming chair sucks Laura into its depths, the hefty cushioning caressing her drained body. She's not ready for a simulation, but it's long overdue—her meeting with Dennis Jenkins. Or Texas, as she's started to call him. To create a feeling of intimacy. Companionship. Friendship. To beat Margaret, she'll need Dennis actively fighting on her side.

Closing her eyes, Laura does her best to ignore the pounding headache in her temples. The AR-glasses resting firmly on her face bring a sensation of security. What a blessing it is that Iris fished them out of the metal can and kept them safe while Laura had her mini breakdown. Margaret had pulled her into the depths of insanity for a moment. The woman had nudged and shoved, poked, and lured, until something in her mind switched off. But no more. That will never happen again. The tables are now about to turn, and with a bit of help from City of California, Laura's going to make sure they turn for good.

The jazz bar is filled with blue lights and lingering smoke. The tables are empty, with candles and ashtrays waiting for customers who will never come. This is a private SIM room—for those with VIP access only. This is nothing like the tacky joints Texas is known to spend his insomnia-filled nights in, luring women half his age.

But this is also not a date. This is a business meeting. The mood is right for the conversation they're about to have. It will be an easy kill: Texas has always had a thing for his employer. Ever since Pharma Salonen became Solomon Foundation, Dennis Jenkins has been a puppy dog, slobbering and bouncing around Laura's feet, begging for scratches and snacks.

And tonight, she'll let the puppy bite.

She strolls through the bar, smooth jazz caressing her tired ears. The update Iris gave her earlier has left Laura wary and weak. If Iris or Nurse Saarinen knew about this meeting, they'd be pissed beyond belief. Tossing around words like exhaustion, overload, and fried cerebrum.

Dennis's Stetson moves to the rhythm of the bass. The man has chosen a corner table, tucked away from curious eyes. Not that there's anyone here; even the bartender is nowhere to be seen. It doesn't matter. The drinks here aren't for drinking. They're for impressing your date with your excellent taste in Spanish wines or your rare knowledge of SIM-whiskeys.

"Evening, dear."

Laura walks to the comfortable-looking armchair in front of Dennis—then sidesteps to sit on the couch beside him. Their knees close to one another, their shoulders brushing slightly, Laura leans over and reaches for the martini glass in front of her. She pretends to take a sip, knowing Dennis is watching her every move.

"Doctor Solomon. What a fantastic sight you are tonight."

She smiles and forces herself not to roll her eyes. Once the glass is back on the table, she gestures at her black dress with its open V-neck. Her white lab coat wouldn't have suited her purpose tonight.

"What, this old thing?"

"Nothing old about you, ma'am."

A genuine laugh. A head tilt. "Well, you know. Fine wine and all that."

"That, indeed."

Laura lets the man's hungry gaze travel over her while she pretends to listen to the live band, which is nowhere to be seen. There are no speakers in the SIM room. No radios or stereos either.

"How have you been?" Dennis asks. "How was The United Inland conference? I was surprised you didn't want me there this time."

"Oh, it was too ordinary and dull for you to bother."

"Nothing's ordinary if you're there."

Dennis has gotten arrogant. Bold. Not too long ago, he had called her Laura. Not Laura Solomon. Not Doctor Solomon. Just Laura. Everyone who works for her knows that Nurse Saarinen is the only one who can do that. And now this. Bold flirting. Hungry eyes, still investigating each mole and freckle on her bare shoulders.

Let him, she reminds herself. *Let him be easily provoked. You need him.*

"Well, dear. As much as I'd love to tell you this little meeting is for us to catch up and get to know one another better, we do have business to attend to."

Dennis leans back in his chair. He hasn't modified his look too much for the simulation, but his thick layer of hair and his flat stomach tell a little white lie. He chews on a toothpick, smiling, at ease. Laura wishes the Texan would be at least a tad nervous about meeting her like this.

"Business, huh?" he says, moving the toothpick from one corner of his mouth to another. "Well . . . " He leans forward and tosses the wooden stick into the ashtray on the table. "The day the boss stops working is the day our world collapses. Can't have that happen, now. Can we?"

Laura smiles at him. "We sure can't."

"What can I do for you?"

"Silverpuffs."

"Yes, sweet cheeks?"

It takes all Laura's willpower not to gag on his supposedly cute joke.

"No, the flowers. What do you know about them?"

"Hmm. I'm afraid I'm not much of a botanist."

"They only grow in California, as far as I know."

"Okay. And?"

"Our mutual friend and fellow founder, Margaret Lewis, is known to hide among them."

"Among silverpuffs? Lewis?"

"That's right."

"Lewis is in California?" Dennis stares at Laura, all flirty comments and tone of voice now gone. "I'll be damned. Would love to find that sneaky fucker."

"I would too. That's why I asked you here tonight. To come up with a plan."

Dennis pops another toothpick into his mouth. For a moment, Laura wonders if he's chewing on one in real life or if it's part of the simulation. She gives the man time to think.

"You know . . ." he says. "I wasn't going to mention it because I was quite heavily whiskey-d that night. But I thought Margaret . . . well, *visited* me."

You conniving piece of shit, she thinks. *Who else's brain have you hacked into?*

"Visited? Really?"

The second toothpick flies into the ashtray. Dennis waves his hand. "I know. How stupid. A grown-ass man hearing things. It might be a good idea for me to spend some time outside these damn rooms." He waves his hand around, gesturing at the simulation. "This and the AR-glasses. I swear, sometimes, I forget which reality is the real one. Sometimes I doubt whether I *know* what is real."

Is Dennis Jenkins losing his mind? Is this a mistake, asking for his assistance to track down their enemy? Then again—Margaret had gotten to Laura as well. The woman had completely thrown her usually calm and collected mind out of whack—twice.

"What did she say?"

"What's that, now?"

"Margaret. When you thought you heard her voice. What did she tell you?"

Dennis folds his hands on his fake-flat belly. His gaze moves from one corner of the room to another as he thinks hard. "Something about home. And the way things once were. She said I could . . ."

"You could what, Texas?" Laura leans closer, staring deep into his eyes. "You can tell me. It's okay."

"She said I could have a family again. A real one. Like I did before Claudia . . . " His voice cracks, and he struggles to continue.

"Right. Before the accident. Listen, dear. What if I were to tell you that it wasn't too much whiskey that pulled that trick on your brain that night? What if I told you it was actually Margaret?"

"Margaret hacked my mind?"

"She did. She hacked mine too. Iris's as well."

Dennis sits taller. He investigates Laura's face, looking for a trace of sarcasm or bad humor, she's sure. "You're not kidding."

"I am not."

"But how is that possible? I'm not one of them."

"You mean Unchipped."

"Right. None of us are."

"It's not really that surprising, her having this know-how. The way she uploaded the virus into the CS and made the Chipped rebels vanish from the system was sensational. At least for someone with her resources, or more accurately her lack thereof. It took us over a month to perfect the override protocol to disassemble the nanobots. And if it weren't for the rebels' own stupidity, it would have taken us even longer to find out where they were."

"Yeah, the resort sure as hell wasn't the first place we looked. Good thing the founders are still on ice. Well, except for your—"

Laura lifts her hand. "That's not why I'm here today. We can discuss my rogue mother some other time. We're here to discuss Margaret's intelligence and the issues it brings."

"So she really did it? Entered my brain and spoke to me?"

She nods. "If she can turn active chips into blind spots, it's not shocking that she can access and control them as well. And now she has."

"I'll be damned."

Laura gives him another moment to gather his thoughts. It is a lot to digest. No one should be there yet—hacking into a chipped brain or communicating through one. The Iceland incident is the closest Laura's come to complete mind control. But the incident is called an incident for a reason: The process is anything but bug-free. Some of the Chipped died, their systems becoming overburdened and finally burning out altogether. Their eyes had glowed with an unnatural light.

The Unchipped, Laura had only been able to put them into a chip-induced coma. It torments her, not knowing the difference between the two. What stops the implant from working in an Unchipped brain?

But her team remains clueless. There's no good reason for the brain receptors to bounce between overactive and extremely low frequencies. The Happiness-Pills have the same impact as coding the nano bots; In an Unchipped brain—they do absolutely nothing. Blockers are the closest thing Laura's team has achieved to understanding these invalid minds, though the effect is short-term and the side-effects can be fatal.

"She figured it out, then?" Dennis asks. "Mind control? Are we in danger?"

Yes.

"No, we are not. There's no way one person alone could achieve such an immense task. Not without a state-of-the-art laboratory and hundreds of scientists working day and night. Lewis has none of these things."

Yet she has successfully hacked into three Chipped minds—maybe more.

"But she was inside my head," Dennis says. "She spoke to me, Laura. In real time. Not in a SIM room, or through the glasses."

"Just a party trick. That's all it was."

A massively, undeniably impressive party trick.

Fishing out a third toothpick to chew on, Dennis folds his arms and lifts his chin. "Well, I don't like it. Not one bit. And isn't Lewis one of them? Chipless?"

"Not Chipless, but Unchipped. And yes. It makes sense that she'd have the ability to tap others of her kind. But she shouldn't be able to tap a Chipped mind."

Dennis huffs. "That's a hell of a party trick, if you ask me."

Laura smiles and reaches for her drink on the table.

"Well. Margaret Lewis is not the only one who can pull a rabbit out of a hat."

"Good. I like that. You have someone who is going to go after her. Fantastic. Who is it?"

Laura brings the martini to her carefully painted lips, takes a sip, and gives Dennis a slight nod.

"You."

The drone hovers above the seemingly abandoned vineyard. The camera feed shows dead crops and a rusty pink van with a sign on top.

MARISCOS Y TACOS

Laura adjusts her AR-glasses and fixes her weight on the gaming chair.

"We have live feed, Texas," she says to her invisible microphone. "Iris is connected and ready to go. How far off are you?"

It takes a few seconds for Dennis to reply.

"Not far at all, Laura."

"Good. Great." She hesitates, pondering her next request. Should she ask Dennis to activate the limousine camera? Laura shakes her head. It's not necessary. But she'd love to see the dark woman sitting next to Dennis, holding a submachine gun. Her brown eyes now glow in an unusual way—or so Dennis had told her when they left City of California's gates and entered the wilderness. "She good?" Laura asks instead. "Under control?"

"My girl's good. Full of piss and vinegar. Ready to rumble."

Nodding, Laura takes a deep breath. "Let's hope we nailed the override this time."

"Wait," Dennis says, "I thought you said she's basically bulletproof?"

"I did say that. And I meant it."

But only when it comes to the override code, she thinks to herself. Maria is Unchipped. If the rechipping operation worked this time, it'd be the first time that has happened . . . ever. Sure, Maria is still standing and operating fine, but if she suddenly started ticking and twitching, Laura wouldn't be terribly shocked. Nurse Saarinen's math has been wrong before.

Things are about to turn ugly up there. Tucked away in what used to be a San Diego mountainside, an underground community of Chipless people hides from surveillance drones and city soldiers. Laura's local crew has been aware of their existence for some time now, but unlike the Unchipped, those without any kind of implant in their brains have never caused any issues in the cities. Eliminating them would have been a simple waste of valuable resources.

Until now.

Margaret is there, among the outsiders. Gazing upon mountains and wildflowers. Hacking into the brain sensors of innocent, upstanding citizens. If it's war the deaf woman wants, it's war she gets.

"Are the sunglasses big enough?" Laura asks. Her heart bounces against her chest, adrenaline rushing through her veins. This has to work. This will work.

"Oh, yes. Big enough to cover that nasty glow. But not too big, so they don't hide her face. The old hag will definitely recognize it's Maria."

Sipping sherry, her mind fully focused on the scene at the remote community near City of California, Laura nearly jumps out of her skin when she hears the girl's voice.

"Doctor Solomon?"

She rips off the glasses and stares at Sanna with wild eyes.

"For the love of . . . " Laura huffs, trying to even out her breathing. "You scared the living hell out of me."

Sanna's sad eyes stare back. She's already wearing her pajama suit. Or maybe she never changed out of it today. Laura's been too occupied with the plan to pay closer attention.

"What is it you need?" Laura asks, forcing a smile. She nods at the gaming chair. "I'm actually a bit busy right now."

"Playing video games?"

"In a way. Yes."

"Do people shoot animals in the game?"

Yes. Filthy, disobedient rebel animals.

"Of course not, sweetie. This is not that kind of game. But it is an important one. Why don't you go back to your room and I'll come tuck you in once the game is over?"

"Is Markus . . . " Sanna's words fade as she reads Laura's expression. She can't help it; it's getting more and more challenging to hide her irritation when it comes to Sanna's strange obsession with the Chipped prisoner.

"I won't be a minute, okay?"

"Okay."

Laura sits back in the chair. Holding the AR-glasses with two hands, she watches Sanna disappear behind the corner, heading for her room at the back of the penthouse. She shoves the AR-glasses on and is just about to ask Dennis what she missed when she sees

Maria. The Unchipped woman who used to work in Texas's mansion walks toward the seating area in front of a beat-down taco stand. Her weapon strapped and hanging from her shoulder, the dark woman's catlike steps take her to a picnic table and old camp chairs.

There's no one around, but Laura can find signs of life everywhere she looks. A coffee mug forgotten in the camp chair's cupholder. Long grass and desert weeds flattened against the ground. A baseball cap, hanging from a nail next to the taco van's serving window.

Maria stops. She stands with her legs parted, looking strong and confident. Laura taps the control panel open, asks the drone to zoom in. If she zooms in close enough, Laura can see the green light pulsing through the small gap between Maria's temples and her sunglasses. Maybe they won't notice. Does it even matter? As long as they get Margaret out alive, Laura couldn't care less what happens to those who have sheltered the traitor. Sheltered her while she viciously hacked into minds no one should ever have been able to enter.

And there she stands. The mindless soldier, pulled out of her capsule and brought back into the daylight only forty-eight hours later. Maria had been shot in an incident that took place in Dennis's mansion late last year. The bullet had passed through Maria, missing all major organs. Laura's crew in City of California's Chip-Center was able to fix her injuries during her rechipping process. Bringing her back was a risk, but Dennis had insisted. He wouldn't shut up about it, ever since Maria was put into a stasis capsule and plugged into the CS.

Now she's back out. Laura had promised Dennis the programming wouldn't fry her brain, like it ended up frying Niina's. The Chipped woman Laura had used in Iceland to protect Sanna and Owena from the takeover had died right after the Solomon Foundation's medical team got over to Iceland. But it had worked, the girls had made it out alive. Niina could have too, it's just that the programming had needed more research time—time that Laura didn't have.

As she zooms out again, a shadow behind the taco stand catches Laura's eye. Maria doesn't move, doesn't say a word. Dennis and his two guards are sitting in a self-driving limo with tinted windows, about forty feet away. The vehicle is locked with a CS-key. It's also bulletproof. If the outcasts have guns, Dennis will be able to flee the scene without anyone important getting hurt.

"Iris, do you see that?" Laura has no idea why she's whispering.

"Movement behind the pink shit-can. Yes, I see it."

"And why isn't the test subject saying anything?"

"She will," Iris mumbles, focused on the task at hand. "There's some disturbance with the connection, but I'm on it."

Dennis chimes in. "Disturbance or not, it's Maria. She was a killing machine even before you turned her into a mindless robot."

"Don't forget, we need—"

"We need Lewis alive, yes, I remember," Iris snaps, clearly needing her full brain capacity to focus on the command codes. Normally, Laura would be insulted at being interrupted, but now she barely notices. Her body's grown tense, and she can barely breathe as she looks at the scene in front of her.

An older woman, closer to seventy than sixty, steps out of the shade. Wild gray hair hangs down around her tanned face, landing on her rugged shoulders. She's wearing a dark-green tank top and cargo pants. Her body seems too fit and strong for a woman her age.

Hawk. That's what Dennis had called her. A Chipless caretaker, running an outcast community in the mountains at an old vineyard. She's known to take a few Unchipped individuals under her wings, though mostly Hawk is all about providing a second chance for those who voluntarily chose a life without chipping.

A compound, Dennis had called the shit-pile they live in. "More like a soup kitchen," Laura had told him, making the man laugh.

The old woman steps closer to Maria. "No guns on the premises, my friend," Hawk says in a loud, clear voice. "But you should already know that, shouldn't you, Maria?"

The soldier doesn't move an inch. A baseball cap covering her shaved head, Maria stands and stares straight at the Chipless leader who used to be her friend. Not a head tilt. No mumble, no heavy breathing, nothing. She just stands and stares.

"This isn't working," Laura says in a low voice. "Where is this disturbance coming from? Iris, can you . . ."

"I haven't forgotten your rules, Hawk." Maria's soft voice interrupts Laura's sentence. Iris must have figured out the issue. Leaning forward in her chair, Laura wishes she could zoom in on both of their faces at once. Has Hawk noticed the neon light in Maria's eyes?

"You always had a good memory." The old woman takes a step forward. "Didn't you, Em?" Without waiting for Maria's response, Hawk nods at the limo nearby. "Nice wheels. You got a promotion or something?"

After a three-second delay, Maria shrugs. "Or something." It's very clear to Laura that it's Iris speaking through Maria, but will Hawk notice?

A young man with a shaved head peeks over Hawk's shoulder. After seeing Maria standing there, he leans in and murmurs something in the leader's ear. Hawk gives him a slight head shake for no.

"Dennis, you seeing this?" Laura whispers.

"Yes, ma'am."

"You're sure they don't have weapons?"

"Positive. If they do, they're tucked away somewhere off-site."

Laura falls silent as the old woman gestures for her crew to stay in the shade, but walks into the open herself. With slow but steady steps, she walks closer to Maria and stops a few feet from her. There, the two women investigate each other. The silence is getting harder and harder to bear.

Finally, a half-smile appears on the older woman's face. "Cool shades."

Maria doesn't react, but her head makes a robotic tweak. Then she's back to normal again.

"Iris, what was that?"

"I got this. Just give me a minute."

"We don't have a minute. If they're trying to hack into our—"

"I said I got it."

With careful sidesteps, Hawk makes her way around Maria and sits at the picnic table. She knocks on a raggedy board twice. "Why don't you sit down, Em? Let Sly-Taco fix us something nice?"

Maria turns in place but doesn't move closer. "I'm afraid this isn't a social call."

Hawk's head tilts, but she doesn't look surprised. "Oh?"

"I'm here to find an old friend. Margaret Lewis. She's needed in the city."

Hawk purses her lips and frowns, clearly pretending to think hard about Maria's words. Then she lifts her chin. "And who is that?"

"Don't play stupid, Hawk. We know she's here with you."

"I'm sorry. *We?*" Again Hawk doesn't look surprised, only acts it. "So let me get this right, Em. Not only did you bring a machine gun to my house. But you brought an outsider as well?"

"Iris, tell her that she brought William to the winery back in the day," Laura says, rushing her words. "That it didn't bother her then."

Maria stands and stares at the woman, a three-second delay in her speech. "But I brought William back in the day. You were okay with him being here."

Hawk stands up and walks over to Maria, stopping only a foot away. "Cut the bullshit, Em. You and I both know it's not Bill sitting in that limo." She reaches for Maria's sunglasses, pulls them off, and tosses them onto the ground. "Just as we know that it's not really Maria who I'm talking with right now. So let's cut to the chase. Who are you, and what do you want?"

Iris moves Maria's hand onto the weapon. She takes a step closer, her glowing eyes now shining straight at the old woman. The tics and head tweaks are getting worse. "I already told you what I want."

Laura's nails sink into the leather of the gaming chair. "Iris, it's time to act. This isn't working. Lure Margaret out now. I don't care how many hobos you need to shoot."

Hawk spreads her hands, looking innocent and calm. "Can't help you there. There's nothing but Chipless people here. Living off the land."

Maria pulls out her submachine gun, pointing it at the taco stand. "And if you don't know who Margaret Lewis is, how do you know that she's not Chipless as well?"

Hawk raises her hands and keeps her eyes fixed on Maria. "I know who she is. And I also know that she's not here."

"Iris, now." Laura holds her breath. Waits.

Three seconds and Maria reacts. "Bullshit." The machine gun fires into the van. The bullets pierce the worn walls and a window shatters. Footsteps thump against the ground as Hawk's people run away from the scene.

"I'll go after them, I swear. I'll hunt them down and kill each and every one of your charity cases."

Hawk stands still, her hands frozen in the air. "I'm sorry. I just can't help you."

Maria fires again. This time, something heavier falls in the shade. Then it's quiet again.

"I'm going to ask you one more time, where—"

"Stop this. Madness."

Laura perks up on the gaming chair. The speech pattern—she knows it by heart.

It's her.

Hawk doesn't turn to look at Margaret but launches herself at Maria, reaching for her weapon. Maria fires for the third time, and the old woman lands lifeless on the ground. The boy with no hair runs over, yelling something in Spanish.

"Shoot him, Iris. Do it now."

Another burst of bullets and the boy lands face down between the picnic tables.

Laura's eyes have never left Margaret.

Eyes watering, Margaret rushes to Hawk's lifeless body. Maria stands still, her weapon now pointing down. Margaret feels for a pulse. Then her chin presses against her chest. A high-pitched cry escapes the deaf woman's throat.

Laura smiles. She's done. Weak. Beaten. Now Dennis just needs to drive her back to the city. Once they have the information they need, Margaret can join William and the other Unchipped scum who now rest in the green city's Chip-Center basement.

The headlights flash twice. A low purr fills the air. Dennis is getting ready to leave the bloodbath and return to his luxury apartment and his nightly adventures in the SIM-dating rooms.

"Time to go," Maria says, walking over to Margaret. The woman ignores her presence, but once Maria grabs hold of her arm, Margaret gets up and leaves her dead ally's side. Maria slings the gun back on her back and pushes Margaret toward their ride. The deaf woman shoves her hands into her pockets, her chin still tucked down, tears flowing down her face.

"Okay, Texas," Laura says, not bothering to hide the excitement in her voice. She taps the video call on, now staring at Dennis's slightly swollen face. "Get me some answers and get them tonight. Nobody rests until she spills the beans."

"Yes, ma'am. You can count on—" Dennis leans closer to the car window. "Hold on. What's going on?"

Laura swipes and taps the air, flicking the drone camera back on. It shows two women walking toward the limousine. Margaret's face is still tucked down, but her hands now cover her eyes, as if to block the sunlight. But it's not sunlight she's hiding from—she's hiding the AR-glasses she's slipped onto her face.

"No, no, no, no. Take the glasses from her, Dennis. Do it now!"

Dennis's heavy breathing fills Laura's ears. He doesn't leave the car.

"Iris, take the glasses. What are you waiting for?"

"The code's not working. Something's blocking my—"

The soldier freezes in place. Iris's voice disappears. Margaret stops too, turns around, and walks over to Maria. The green glow in her eyes is gone. The tics, her robotic gestures. All gone. The woman dressed in black looks confused, then horrified, as reality enters her previously hijacked mind.

"Dennis, get out of that car and fix this!"

More heavy breathing. Laura stands up, pacing around the apartment, her hands ripping at her hair. "For fuck's sake! Somebody do *something*!"

Margaret supports Maria by her shoulders, turning the woman away from the sight of her dead friends. She takes off her AR-glasses, reaches for Maria's weapon, and wraps her arm around the now crying and shaking woman. Then she starts walking toward the limo.

Laura's hands freeze on her temples. She stares at the camera feed, shaking her head rapidly. "Don't you dare move that car, Dennis." She kicks the gaming chair and raises her voice. "Don't you dare leave."

The heavy breathing stops as the audio from the vehicle is blocked. Margaret now stands only a few feet from Dennis and his men—pointing the machine gun straight at them.

"It's bulletproof, Dennis. Stay put."

The car keeps purring with all its lights on.

"You designed the fucking thing yourself! There's nothing this bitch can do to hurt you."

The car starts backing up down the dirt road.

"Dennis! You useless shit!"

As the vehicle slowly departs, Maria snaps out of her shock. She takes the gun from Margaret and starts running after the black limo. Rapid fire cracks and pops in Laura's ears as she watches her plan shatter into pieces—unlike the self-driving car, which escapes the scene without a scratch on its shiny surface.

Laura sits back down on the gaming chair, out of breath, too stunned to be furious yet. She stares at the woman. The traitor. The bane of her existence. But Laura can stare all she wants, Margaret's still out of her reach.

Maria turns slowly, then gazes up to the sky where the drone still hovers. Her scream echoes around the open yard. Once the bullets reach the sky, a neon-blue error message appears in front of Laura's eyes.

*OOPS! THERE SEEMS TO BE A GLITCH IN
YOUR HAPPINESS-PROGRAM.
PLEASE TRY AGAIN LATER.*

The bunny's whiskers tickle the back of Laura's hands. Sitting on the floor, she strokes Mister Bun-Bun's long ears, enjoying the animal's weight and warmth against her pajama-covered thighs. A low humming fills the bedroom. The song is familiar, something from the time before The Great Affliction. A Finnish children's song. She wonders whether Markus can't remember the words or if he just prefers humming.

How long has she sat here? It must be midnight, maybe later. Sanna's scream had snapped her out of her rage and disappointment after they lost Maria to Margaret. Iris is still downstairs at the lab. Not that Laura's checked if she's there. She doesn't need to. The Icelandic woman had been just as upset about the mission going south as Laura.

Markus smooths the blanket over the sleeping Sanna and gets up slowly. With silent footsteps, he walks over to Laura. His shoulders sag a little and there are dark circles under his eyes, telling Laura that the Chipped prisoner hasn't gotten the best sleep as of late. How could he have? Four nights out of five, he has to come up to the penthouse and comfort a screaming kid who never agrees to share her nightmares with anyone. Or at least not with Laura.

"She's out cold," Markus says. "I'd like to return to my box now."

Laura's laugh is tired but genuine. "That's hardly true, dear. That would mean you like living in the basement." Laura fixes her seat, careful not to startle the bunny that rests on her lap. "At least this prisoner seems much happier up here than he would be in a glass box."

Markus folds his arms. "Good for him. I guess not all of us are worthy of your pity."

"Who said anything about pity?"

"Why else would you let the bunny live?"

Laura's hand rests on the creature's soft hair. "Of course I'm letting him . . ." Laura stops. "Why does everyone think I'm some sort of bunny-slaughtering monster?"

Markus gestures for Laura to keep her voice down. It had taken him hours to get Sanna back to sleep. Laura scowls at him but continues running her fingers on the silky coat. "I would never hurt something Sanna cares for so deeply."

Her words get Markus's attention. He unfolds his arms and sits down on the floor, four feet away from Laura and Mister Bun-Bun. "And what makes Sanna so special? Why is it that all the other Unchipped—adults and kids—now rest inside those hell-pods, but she's up here with you?"

He's crossed a line. Asking questions that are none of his business. But for some reason, it makes Laura respect Markus more. Maybe the Chipped rebel is not totally spineless after all.

"We're connected from the time before," she tells him. "That's all you need to know."

"Did you know her parents?"

Laura laughs again, feeling more and more drained by the minute. Her hand rubs the bunny's neck gently. "Yes, dear. I guess you could say that. Not so much her father, but Sanna's mother and I were like two peas in a pod."

"What was she like?"

Laura investigates Markus's face, trying to figure out why he cares. One day she'll be able to read people's minds, and there'll be no room for wonder. But right now, the man with overgrown hair remains a mystery to her. And though she hates that the thought crosses her mind, she can kind of understand why Sanna finds his company so soothing.

"Not sure I remember much about Sanna's mother. It's been ten years."

"Was she Unchipped?"

Laura gives him a half-smile. "Definitely not Unchipped. She was one of the first to get chipped, actually."

The first one, she adds in her mind.

"So she was important then? Did she work for you?"

"She worked for my mother. Mrs. Salonen. I believe you met in Iceland?"

Unstartled by the unpleasant memory—the Iceland incident—Markus doesn't dodge Laura's stare. "We met briefly, yes. Not that I had the chance to talk to her." He narrows his eyes. "Would have been interesting to hear what she did to deserve being stored away like that. And by her own daughter."

Laura shrugs. "Save your judgment, dear. My mother was a lot of things, but she was far from perfect. Sure, thanks to her, we now have stasis capsules, chipping helmets, and Happiness-Pills. But she never had it in her to create a more advanced world."

"A world where people are turned into useless vegetables?"

"Now, dear, I wouldn't call the good people that. They work very hard, and I don't mean just those who pedal or the gardeners at the Vertical Farming-Center. This city is what started it all. It makes our society what it is today. An example of a better tomorrow. So what if it's done with pills and brain augmentation? How is that any different from psychotherapy and antidepressants? You wouldn't believe how many Finns were dependent on both when The Great Affliction happened. The whole country was dependent on our government's health care and still these people barely hung on. Trust me, I still have access to the national health records. It's all there, every single symptom, every Euro spent trying to save people who would never work a day in their lives. Numb, broken, useless. Costing us money just by existing. And boom, look at them now—"

"Thank you for this history lesson, Doctor. But that's not what I meant when I said you're turning people into useless vegetables."

Laura smiles at him and sighs. "Aha. You're referring to the people in the capsules. But they're hardly useless, dear. Without the processing power they provide, the AR-city could never run as smoothly as it does today. Our Super CS-key is being developed every day, but it still only has the processing power of eight capsuled people."

"Eight people, eight hundred people . . . doesn't matter. It's just not right."

"Even if it's for their own good?"

"You are not a god. You shouldn't act like one."

She gives him a warm smile. "I see. So, it's only okay for your little crew to decide who gets to live and who doesn't?"

"What?"

"Your little scheme in Iceland? The kill switch that would open all the capsules in the city?"

"Those people should have a choice."

"Those people would all have died if I had let you proceed with your plan."

Markus stares at her, opening his mouth to say something . . . but then decides against it. He's probably contemplating whether Laura is telling him the truth. Which she is.

"See, my dear . . . Proper function of this level of nanobot load is not sustainable or survivable outside of the capsule system." Her motherly smile deepens. "Ah, but you know all this already. Because of your friend from City of Serbia. What's her name again . . . " Her index finger taps her chin lightly. "Sloanne? Slowena?"

"Sloboda."

"Ah, yes. Lady Freedom. Anyway . . . " She tilts her head, investigating Markus's face in the dim room. "If the subject is removed from the capsule before the system flushes the additional nanobots, their body function is severely impacted, causing stroke, embolism, and massive organ failure."

"She didn't die because we took her out." Unsure, Markus looks away. "She had cancer."

"Mm. Yes, she did when she was first put into the capsule. But by the time you removed her the cancer should have been long gone. Did I say it happens instantly? It can happen quite rapidly afterward, or later on. Your friend would have lived, if she had stayed in the capsule and had been removed following the proper procedure. Reverend Marić knew this. Why else would he have brought his wife to us?"

Markus swallows but doesn't answer.

"You must understand . . . When removed improperly, a subject's life expectancy is less than a month at the most, but may become terminal within one or two days or sooner depending on the state of their overall health and the repair of the initial ailment. And how long did your friend last?"

He lowers his gaze.

"Two weeks? A month?"

Nothing.

"I mean, she would have lasted awhile. Being in a healing capsule for so long would have left her quite healthy. She would be dancing around the purple city as we speak, if it wasn't for . . . " She waves him off, deciding he's suffered enough for now. "Well, you know what you did."

Finally, dodging her gaze, the man shakes his head slowly and murmurs to himself.

"What's that, dear?"

He looks up again, eyes filled with hate. "Doesn't change a thing. Any of what you just said. You're still wrong. About everything. We only wanted to help. To do the humane thing. You, on the other hand . . ." He nods at the bunny on Laura's lap. "You'd kill that rabbit in a nanosecond. If it benefited or profited you in any way."

Grabbing the bunny under its chubby belly, Laura lifts the rabbit to eye level. "You know . . . this little guy and my mother have more in common than not." After staring into the critter's little face for a while, Laura places it carefully on the floor. The bunny freezes between Laura and Markus, unsure of which way to hop. "They're both prey animals. Soft. Weak. Trying to remain invisible in a world where being visible will destroy you. And you know what? She was like that too, ten years ago."

"Who was?"

Laura's gaze travels to the sleeping girl, tucked under multiple blankets. "Sanna's mother," she says. "She was held back by those who try to rule the world with a soft hand and compromise. But not anymore. She will never make the mistake of listening to someone else ever again."

"So she's still alive?"

Laura's eyes drill into Markus. "No," she says. "She's long gone. And trust me, it's better that way."

They sit in silence, both lost in their own thoughts. After what seems like a small eternity, Markus gets up from the floor.

"Well. As much fun as this little chat has been . . . " Markus takes a few steps but stops when his movement startles Mister Bun-Bun. The bunny runs into his carrier next to Sanna's bed. "I've got a date with a nurse and an elevator."

Laura looks at the rabbit, then at the sleeping girl, then at Markus's back as he nears the door. "Hold on," she says, not moving a muscle to get up from the floor.

His hand on the doorknob, Markus turns to face Laura.

"Why don't you sleep up here tonight?" Laura asks. "Not in the penthouse, but there's a free room down-stairs, next to Nurse Saarinen's apartment."

Markus frowns. "Why on earth would you give me a room up here?"

Laura shrugs. "Because I'm not a bunny killer. And I'm willing to prove it. Does it profit me in any way? Letting you sleep in a comfy bed and live a little? No. Does it benefit me tomorrow morning when you 3D print yourself a grab-a-cup and a nice blueberry muffin? All in the comfort and privacy of your very own room? Not in the slightest. But I'll let you do it anyway."

"Why?"

"Maybe I like you."

"You don't like anyone but yourself."

When Laura doesn't answer, just leans her head against the wall with a tired smile on her face, Markus leaves the room. Will he stay? Ask Nurse Saarinen to take him to his new digs? Nurse Saarinen would believe him, of course. Lying about such a privilege would be out of character for him.

The door shuts behind him.

Laura sits in the dimly lit room, listening to Sanna's even breath. The bunny chews on a piece of hay, then jumps over to the other side of its carrier to drink. The small metal ball inside the drink bottle rattles loudly as Mister Bun-Bun takes tiny gulps.

"Cute. Creature."

Laura presses her eyes shut.

Not again.

She takes a deep breath, trying to relax her body and mind. No need to react. No need to panic. She had known Margaret would be back. Overriding Maria's programming so rapidly only proves her power over them. She's still two steps ahead.

"He's called Mister Bun-Bun. Not the most creative name, but it'll grow on you."

"I'm. Sure. It will."

Laura gets up from the floor and follows Markus's footsteps out the door. She walks down the corridor into the living room, pours herself a glass of sherry. "So, did she make it?"

"Maria?"

"Mm." Laura takes more than a sip, hoping the alcohol will slow down the adrenaline rush of having someone hijack her brain.

"She's recovering. Still in shock."

Laura raises her eyebrows, pours herself a refill. "So, we didn't fry her brain?" She takes a quick sip and walks toward the gaming chair, eyeing her AR-glasses. "That's an improvement."

"Your programming. Wasn't. Ready. Laura."

"That's Doctor Solomon to you."

"You can't. Just. Test drive. People. Laura."

Irritation washes away the uncomfortable sensation of someone invading her mind. "Like I said. It's Doctor Solomon to you." Her voice remains calm and deep. "And I can do whatever the fuck I want."

For a moment, everything is quiet. Laura moves her head around, rubs her neck and stretches her jaw like she's trying to get rid of a neck spasm. She drinks the sherry and squeezes the empty glass in her hand. Lifting her chin, speaking one word at a time, she adds, "You. Arrogant. Deaf. Bitch."

The sensation is overwhelming. It sweeps through her, raising goosebumps all over her body. Before Laura understands what's happening, she watches her hand rise above her head, still holding the sherry glass. She tries to move her legs but can't. She tries to lower her hand but can't. Her legs, her feet, her head. Nothing.

"For years. I've. Watched you. Play. God."

Words stuck in her throat, Laura watches her pinky finger let go of the glass.

"How you. Dictate and ruin. A cause. That your mother. Once created."

Her ring finger separates from the glass surface. Laura tries to scream, but the lump in her throat muffles the sound.

"How you. Degrade. Torture. Murder."

The rest of her fingers open, sending the glass plummeting toward the floor. Glass shards shatter all around her feet, some of them landing on her slippers. Her hand is stuck above her head, her voice silenced by Margaret's hostile takeover. A tingling pain in her left foot makes her want to look down, but she still can't move her head.

"Unnerving. Isn't it?"

A groan is all Laura can manage.

"Now imagine. If I did. What you did. To Maria."

Her hand drops down, pulling Laura's shoulder painfully out of whack. Moving her head is still hard, and her whole body seems to be paralyzed. But she's still standing. Then, her feet start to move. Laura watches how her slightly bloody left foot takes a step forward, missing the biggest pieces of glass. Then the right foot follows. Then the left. And the right. Soon she's walking along the corridor toward Sanna's room.

"Sss," Laura hisses and tries to fight the force that keeps her from talking. Then she stops just outside Sanna's bedroom door, her hand on the knob.

"Imagine. If I. Made you. Hurt."

Laura's hand opens the door, but her feet stay put, bleeding on the floor.

"Phh . . ."

"For the longest. Time. I thought you. Just didn't. Understand. That you wouldn't. Know what. Love. Is."

Laura fights against the commands in her brain. She won't walk in. She won't hurt the sleeping girl. No code or program could be strong enough.

"But then. I saw you. Going after. Her. After all. These. Years."

Laura watches her hand pull the door shut. "Sh . . . " Her feet turn her back to the corridor, her legs move steadily, this time toward the penthouse balcony. As if in a dream, she watches herself slide the door aside—and step outside to a narrow balcony she's never visited in her life.

The door shuts behind her with a smooth *thud*.

"So maybe. You are. Capable of. Love. And therefore. You must also. Know. Fear."

Her body moves closer to the railing. Heart racing wildly against her chest, Laura tries to close her eyes so she won't be able to see the drop down. The familiar dizziness, her fear of heights, mixes with the nauseating sensation of losing control over her own body.

Her hands grab onto the metal rail. Laura watches herself climb onto the railing, one leg at a time, then flip her body over. Feet wobbling, hands wrapped around the metal, she blinks rapidly, trying not to look down.

Her chin tucks against her chest. She's forced to look down.

The blue tile roads and billboards glimmer in the night. A lonely hologram flickers on and off next to the Chip-Center courtyard. It's a long way down. She's so high up that if she could move her head and gaze over at the horizon, she'd see the forest and wilderness beyond the stone wall that surrounds her city.

Her stomach flips. A hot, sour taste fills her mouth as Laura vomits all over herself.

"So you are. A human. After all."

"Stop this." Suddenly, she's able to speak. But the fear of falling makes her voice shake. It would make her body tremble as well, if it wasn't frozen solid by Margaret's malware. "Let's talk . . ." A gag interrupts Laura's sentence as bile floods her mouth. " . . . like civil human beings."

"Civil? Like you were. In California. Killing all. Those innocent. People?"

A drop of blood trails from her left foot. Laura watches it disappear into the blue-black night.

"Just let me down, Margaret."

"Poorly. Chosen. Words."

Her right foot slips off the railing and hangs swinging in the air.

"No! Pl . . ." The lump returns, suffocating Laura's scream.

The city starts to spin around her. Neon lights, high buildings, billboards, and holograms race in front of her eyes. Images of Sanna laughing. Bunny whiskers. Snake tongues. A dead body shoved inside a small glass box. Her head feels like it's being compressed; she's about to lose consciousness.

Flitting in and out of consciousness, Laura feels like her body's starting to float. Maybe she's falling, soon to crash on the blue tiles. Too exhausted to be scared, she lets go, relaxes against the feeling of nothingness. Finally, she's able to close her eyes.

Floating against the bottom of the sea. The water humming around her. A caressing hand stroking her head. It's comforting, being dead. Freeing. But cold. Like the winter nights in her childhood. Snowflakes drilling into her skin, sending shivers down her spine.

"Laura."

Why is Margaret still here? This is Laura's death. Her forever after.

"Laura. Wake. Up."

Blurry and unfocused, her eyes take in the scene. A metal railing. A blue glow mixing with the light of the rising sun. The city's about to wake up to a new day.

She never fell. She's not dead after all.

"Why didn't you . . . " Laura breathes out, her tongue too large to fit in her mouth. Everything aches; her toes, her stomach, her hair. She moves her head, then her fingers. She's in control. Her body is numb, but it's hers again.

"Why didn't. I. Kill you?"

Laura gasps for air, then turns flat against the balcony wall. Slowly she moves toward the open sliding door, then crawls inside. With both hands, she slides the door shut and crashes against the penthouse floor. "Yes," she breathes out, her cheek pressed against the cool floor. "Why did you let me live?"

Margaret's still with her, lingering somewhere at the back of Laura's mind. She can feel her presence, the aftershock shaking her body. It feels like she's been frozen for years, now slowly melting and coming back to life.

"*I would. Never. Kill you. Laura.*"

She blinks, enjoys the feeling of a solid floor under her body.

"You should have," she then says, her voice back to its normal robust tone. "Because I'll never stop."

Margaret's presence keeps fading away. "*I won't. Kill you. Because. I'm not. You.*" Margaret's calm voice booms in Laura's ears long after she's gone. "*You and I. Are. Nothing. Alike.*"

CHAPTER 5

WALKING ON EGGSHELLS

Staring at the printed paper Iris holds in her hands, Laura supports herself against the lab desk next to her. It's like having the hangover of a lifetime, coming out of whatever it is Margaret did with her chip last night. Focusing on Iris's words is hard. Just standing here, trying to look sharp, is overwhelming.

Iris waves at the paper. "Did you hear me, Doctor Solomon?"

Eyes blank, Laura's gaze flickers between Iris's eyes and the document in her hand.

"I said . . . "

"Yes." Laura shakes her head and stands taller. Slowly, she lets go of the wall to balance her aching body on her own. Did Margaret also give her some sort of a beating? While she was out cold on the balcony floor? "Someone used the 3D printer to send us a paper sheet with information. And then you asked,

'What's next, a fax?'" Laura moves her toes around carefully, wondering how obvious it is that she's in pain. "So yes, I heard you."

Iris and Nurse Saarinen exchange a look. Their teams hover nearby, waiting to hear about the mysterious paper that appeared on the printer's tray overnight. Nurse Saarinen glances around and raises her eyebrows at the curious onlookers, sending everyone back to work.

Iris walks over to Laura. "It's not just any information. Doctor, if this is true, we'll know the difference between—"

"You know it's a mindfuck. She's messing with us," Laura interrupts her.

"What?"

"Who uses a 3D printer to print out a paper sheet?"

Nurse Saarinen joins them and snaps the paper from Iris's hands. "It's not a mindfuck, it's a scam. Something to do with Lewis, for sure. I say we tear it up. Why would we let that maniac mess with us any more than she already has?"

The memory of her leg swaying in the night wind forces Laura to sit down. She buries her head in her hands, then rubs her eyes and temples for a time before replying. Gazing through her fingers, Laura looks at Iris's frowning face. "And what do you suggest?"

"Normally, I'd agree with Nurse Saarinen." Iris pauses to glance at Nurse Saarinen as she scoffs sarcastically at her words. "However," she takes a step closer to Laura, "these calculations are way too interesting for us to ignore. Whoever sent this—"

"Lewis sent it, and you know it," Nurse Saarinen says, tapping her foot against the lab floor.

"Even so, if this is real, it explains why we haven't been able to figure out the Unchipped brain. See, we've been focused on the brain receptors and the nano bots not working correctly. How they're immune to the code commands as well as any chemicals that activate nerve impulses in a Chipped brain. But what if it's more to do with the electrical impulses—"

"That's idiotic." Nurse Saarinen hands the paper back to Iris. "We've tried deep brain stimulation through electrodes multiple times on hundreds of test subjects."

"True. But we did it without balancing the frequency first. With HSP a person's sensory processing isn't the same. Look." Iris places the paper on the table in front of Laura. "If this is right—"

"And not some fucked up scam," Nurse Saarinen adds.

Iris closes her eyes to take a deep breath. "If this is right, we've been approaching the issue backward. We can fix the chip and the nano bots all day long…"

"... but it won't take because of their hypersensitivity to stimuli," Laura says. She stares at the chart below a long code she can't read. Why would Margaret share this information with them?

"I can't believe you two would fall for this," Nurse Saarinen says. She grabs the paper from the table to read it again. "It's too easy. If this is accurate, it means that the Unchipped are just highly sensitive people. And the research on HSP is speculative at best."

Iris nods at the paper. "It's not as simple as them being sensory sensitive. This is a frequency we're not familiar with."

"What's the code?" Laura asks, tuning out Nurse Saarinen's scoffs. "Will it fix the issue? No more Unchipped people?"

"Give me an hour. I will let you know then."

Nurse Saarinen laughs and folds her arms. "Unbelievable. You think Margaret just came to her senses overnight? Sends us a cake and lets us eat it too?" She raises her hands. "Well, I'm not biting. Whatever that code is, it's poisonous. Probably another virus and this time it'll shut down our system for good."

Iris sits down, AR-glasses now covering her eyes. Her fingers start moving on the invisible keyboard, her mind absent from their conversation.

Nurse Saarinen now stares at Laura, shaking her head slowly as she waits for an explanation.

"What?" Laura says after getting up from her seat and nodding at the 3D printer in the corner of the lab. "Can you vent at me by the coffee, please? I didn't get much sleep last night."

Nurse Saarinen follows her to the lab's small kitchen area.

"About that." Nurse Saarinen nods in the direction of the glass rooms. "Why is that poorly groomed rebel suddenly sleeping in a room next to my apartment?" She watches Laura insert a plastic coffee mug under the printer nozzle. "I hope you at least hid all the sharp objects from our floor before you handed him a set of pajamas and a key."

"Markus won't do anything to hurt you." Laura brings the steaming cup to her lips and blows on the coffee. "Trust me."

Nurse Saarinen bites her lip. Flustered and confused, she looks like she's having a hard time watching her words. She doesn't agree with Laura, but Laura's still in charge.

"That code. And this unknown frequency," Nurse Saarinen says at last. "What makes you think Margaret would help us chip people all of a sudden? And who's to say if Lewis even sent this?"

Laura takes a careful sip of coffee. The liquid burns her tongue, but she takes another sip anyway. "I don't think she is helping us figure out the chipping process."

"No?"

"No," Laura says, shaking her head once. "She's Unchipped herself. Or maybe a hybrid at this point. Who knows. But whatever she is, she's not on our side."

"So it's a scam."

Laura empties the cup in few long gulps. The liquid burns on its way down.

"Not a scam, not really. But a mindfuck for sure." Laura places the mug back into the 3D printer and presses a button. "I think she's trying to prove that the Unchipped are not the problem, but the solution."

"The solution to what? To humanity eating its own tail?" Nurse Saarinen huffs. "And you're falling for this nonsense? You believe her now?"

Laura holds onto the coffee cup, letting it burn her fingers.

"Not for one second."

The Unchipped woman lies on the operating table, her blond hair tucked under a chipping helmet. A scar travels from her cheek to her jawline, then down to her collarbone. Laura stares at it, lost in her thoughts. Despite the fact that Nurse Saarinen's chipping crew is watching her, waiting to get started, Laura runs her finger along the mark.

"I heard it was that one," Nurse Saarinen says and nods at a stasis capsule a few feet away from the operating table where a broad-shouldered man rests under his chipping helmet, "who carved her skin."

Laura's head jerks back in surprise. She turns to look at the man they brought from Iceland. The soldiers had found him and Kaarina curled up together in the resort kitchen.

"Him? That's unlikely. I think the two were some sort of item."

Nurse Saarinen snorts. "Go figure. Romance is on the verge of extinction, yet these rebel morons are too pig-headed to let it go. The idea that they're somehow special or significant is just so far-fetched. Like humans being able to raise their own children."

She takes a quick step forward, winces, and stops. Her feet are still sore, maybe even bleeding. With more careful steps, Laura walks over to the man in the capsule. Scars smaller than Kaarina's mark his sharp face. His broad chest is covered with sandy brown curls that match the color of his hair where it sticks out from under the chipping helmet.

"Do you think she's a real threat?" Laura half-whispers, temporarily mesmerized by these creatures. They seem more like a pack of wolves than human beings.

"It's probable. Kaarina wasn't always part of the Unchipped community. She lived alone somewhere near the suburbs. Before she became a rebel leader. People don't generally survive alone like that, so I'd say she has the means."

And stole my daughter from me, Laura adds in her mind. More than once, Iris has offered to erase the memory from Laura's mind. How the Chipped turned against her. Kidnapped her daughter. First escaping the city, then attacking it. After everything she has done for them over the years, these ungrateful low-lifes had no respect. And they still won't. That's why the rebel Chipped are held in the glass rooms or in stasis capsules until further notice.

"Doctor Solomon? Shall we begin?"

It's the head neurosurgeon talking. Emilia Keskitalo. Laura nods at her. Then she turns away from them both—the mountain of a man and his rebel girlfriend.

"That's what you get, dear Kaarina," Laura murmurs as she watches the screens behind the chipping helmet flicker to life. "First, you got your face sliced. Now, it's your brain's turn."

She nods at the crew. "Don't worry if the test subject doesn't make it. Scan the frequency as efficiently as you can. If we lose this one," Laura points at the scar-faced man's stasis capsule, "continue with that one."

She turns to walk away. But she doesn't get far.

The sudden inability to control her legs knocks Laura off her feet. A ringing sound in her ears, she stares at the base of a stasis capsule as she lies paralyzed on the floor. Muffled footsteps echo around her, but she can hardly hear them. Someone grabs her by the shoulders and shakes her, but she can't turn her head to see who it is.

"Don't touch her. Step away," Iris's panicked voice seems to come from under water. "Go get me a chipping helmet and my CS-key. Now!"

"What's wrong with her?" Nurse Saarinen's nasal voice pierces through the ringing sound as it slowly turns into a pounding thud. Laura's unsure if it's her own heartbeat she's listening to, or the woman who has re-entered her mind without permission.

"She's been hacked."

"Fuck me. Lewis?"

"Who else."

Laura feels intense pressure around her skull as the chipping helmet locks in. The pounding sound pulls her deeper into a state of mind she's never experienced before. It's like being stuck in an empty SIM room. She looks around her, but all she can see are endless white walls.

"Your. Mother."

Margaret's voice is so close to her, it feels like her own. Like Laura is repeating her words, not just listening to them.

"You can't do this to me."

Margaret doesn't answer right away. While waiting, Laura feels as if she's floating in the air, her body limp and numb.

"You know. What. Your mother. Would say?"

Laura doesn't reply. She focuses on her breathing, suddenly worried that if she doesn't, her body will refuse to take another breath to keep her alive.

"She'd say. That it's. Like you're. Stuck. Inside an egg."

The white walls. This is insanity.

"I thought you said . . . " Laura has to stop and breathe. "You said you wouldn't kill me."

"I did. And I. Won't."

"They'll go on without me. You can't save her. Kaarina's done."

Margaret's silhouette appears in the distance. A mirage above the white floor moves in sync with her footsteps. Like hot air on a paved road, the woman seems to float above nothing. Then, white hair and a familiar face appear. And the face doesn't belong to Margaret. The woman smiles and kneels down next to Laura, then lies beside her, staring deep into her eyes.

"Hey, sweetie."

Laura blinks but can't move. She stares at the wrinkles around her face. Stares at the soft eyes that used to frustrate her beyond anything else.

"I guess you're not dead after all, mother."

Gazing deep into her mother's eyes, Laura has lost the concept of time. All pain has left her body. It disappeared as soon as she stopped fighting her paralyzed state. Floating in the nothingness, Mrs. Salonen's hand stroking her head, she lies there and listens to the silence they're wrapped in.

She could be dead. The thought does enter her mind, but Laura fails to care. It feels good to let go. Just to be. Unattached from her responsibility to save the world and the creatures that flounder in it.

"Why do you hate them so much?" Laura whispers.

Her mother's lips twitch, deepening the smile on her face. "Hate whom, sweetie?" She adjusts her wrinkly hand underneath her cheek but goes on stroking Laura's hair. "I don't think I've ever hated another living being. I don't think I would know how."

"Not people, Mother."

"What then?"

"White walls. Why do you hate them so much?"

When Mrs. Salonen laughs, the creases around her face become clearer. Even this old, she's mesmerizingly beautiful. A glow that Laura's always seen on her face seems to become even more distinct in this odd space they lie in.

"I don't hate white walls, either."

"Sure you do."

She cups her hand around Laura's cheek, pauses to think—then continues to pat Laura's head.

"I just prefer color. Orange, green, red, even black. Contrast is what makes life interesting. Two opposites finding a way to mix with each other. Blend in. Black stripes on a white surface–or is it white stripes on black?"

"Black isn't really a color."

She shrugs and smiles at Laura. "Just as an egg is not really white. Not completely."

"Right. The vitelline membrane. Is that what we're supposed to be right now? Two unborn chicks about to be eaten? That's cute, Mother."

Laura can't help it. Her mother's laughter makes her smile.

"Such an incredible imagination. You've always had it, sweetie."

"Must have gotten that from you."

"Oh?"

Laura moves her head under her mother's touch, surprised to notice she has full control over her body. She could stand up and run. Leave the old woman lying here alone to pat imaginary unborn chicks. But where would she go?

"It takes a lot of creativity," Laura continues, "to maintain your blind faith in humanity. Especially when it's committing suicide in front of your eyes."

Mrs. Salonen's happy grin turns into a half-smile.

"We're all flawed, Laura. Even you."

"Of course I am flawed. If I'd done everything perfectly, I wouldn't be lying here with you. Hijacked."

"Have you ever considered that this is what the people in the capsules feel like? Like this, but with no one to talk to?"

"You're expecting an apology?" Laura laughs a little, rolling her eyes. "Do you even know what your time in the capsule did for your life expectancy?"

Her mother shrugs. "Did wonders for my hip, sure. But it wasn't exactly a restful beauty nap, either."

"Mind mapping has come quite a long way since you last entered a Chip-Center, Mother. We do frequent scans before we plug into the CS for processing power. Those people can't think or feel a thing. Complete anesthesia."

"Is that what you call an apology?"

"You'll never hear me apologize for fixing what was broken."

"And the Unchipped?"

Laura lifts her hand to push the caressing fingers off her head.

"What about them?"

"You can't monitor their brains."

"Sure I can."

"But not the way you would monitor a Chipped or chip-free brain."

"I can still monitor their bodily functions. They're not in pain."

"Physical pain is hardly the only pain there is. And it's not the worst kind, either. Laura, you need these people just as much as they need you. There's something special about them and the way they interact with others. An Unchipped brain is so high-functioning, it can block us from rewriting it. Imagine what these people could do if we could learn from them—"

"Mother, they are an anomaly in the system. Nothing more. Nothing less. Being high-functioning doesn't automatically mean high IQ. Wouldn't you rather sacrifice a few worker ants, if it saves the whole colony? This is your problem; it always has been. You romanticize instead of searching for a solution. You want to believe that these people are the key to our existence because you've been unable to figure out what's wrong with them."

"True. Though you're forgetting one thing."

"What's that?"

"I've been stuck in a stasis capsule for most of it."

Laura takes a deep breath. "Doesn't matter. Because I know you. You've always had a soft spot for the weak, and that makes you vulnerable and foolish."

"No, sweetie. That's not—"

"You paint the walls in pretty colors, instead of facing the fact that pure white makes you anxious and mad."

Eyes watering, Mrs. Salonen tucks both of her hands under her head. They lie there in silence, Laura fighting the tears that burn her eyes too. Why should she cry? She's not the one who should be sad or desperate. She's not the one who has wasted her life's work trying to fix things that are beyond repair.

A teardrop falls from Laura's eye. It falls down into the abyss, disappearing into its white nothingness. Her mother's hand twitches, but she resists the urge to comfort her child.

Then the ringing sound returns. Hard. Piercing. Drilling into Laura's mind and shaking her body as the sound turns into a pulling and ripping agony. She holds her head, gasping for air and curling up into a fetal position.

"Laura, what's wrong?"

"Iris . . ." She pauses to gasp for air. "She's bringing me back."

"Laura, listen to me. Don't update the guards. Don't block me out. We need to talk . . . until . . . through . . . solution . . . " Her mother's voice is breaking up. The agony of being ripped between two realities is too much for Laura to open her eyes and see if her mother is still there.

"Wait for . . . and measure . . . frequency . . . cure."

The ringing stops just as quickly as it began. All pain is gone, but a tingling sensation now envelops her body. It's like she's slept on her arm too long, but instead of an arm, it's her whole body that needs better blood flow.

"Doctor Solomon, can you hear me?" A hand carefully touches her shoulder. Without opening her eyes, Laura wishes the hand would pet her hair—caressing, loving. "She's not responding, Iris. You did it wrong."

"Did what wrong? You don't even know what it is I do."

"Well, just because I'm not a coder—"

"You're a fucking nurse."

"A neuroscientist."

"Whatever. It worked. She just needs time."

Nurse Saarinen's voice comes closer. She must have leaned over Laura to whisper. It's just that she has no idea how to do so. "Laura, you with us?"

Laura moves her head farther away from the high-pitched sound and opens her eyes. Iris spreads her hands and exhales deeply.

"I'm here. I'm fine." Laura tries to get up, but her head seems to be glued to the floor. At least five people rush over to her. One of them removes the chipping helmet from her head, the rest help her sit upright. Iris kneels next to Laura, her eyes flickering from Laura's eyes to her CS-key and back.

"Must have been one hell of a trip."

"It was. I feel like an omelet."

"What?"

"Nothing."

Laura moves her feet, then starts to get up from the floor. When the people around her move in to help, she raises her hand and gestures for them to back off. Slowly, supporting herself against a stasis capsule, Laura pushes her body up. The room spins, but only for a while. Taking deep breaths, she stares through the tinted glass of a capsule, where an old woman rests peacefully. For a moment, Laura imagines the test subject's smooth brown skin changing into a pale face with deep creases.

"Talk to me, Laura," Nurse Saarinen says beside her. "What do you need?"

The old woman in the capsule changes again. She is clearly not Laura's mother. Maybe Laura only dreamed her. Maybe Mrs. Salonen was never there.

"I think I'm going to have an early night," Laura says.

"It's ten forty-five in the morning," a man says behind her back. Nurse Saarinen gives him a dirty look. Soon footsteps thump against the lab floor as the team scatters to give them space.

Iris clears her throat and places her hand on Laura's shoulder. "Take as much time as you need. We have everything under control here."

"Agreed. The coder and I will send you a report once we've sliced up the first test subject. If the frequency scaling won't give us what we need, that is."

Laura blinks rapidly. "You're still going forward with Kaarina?"

Iris and Nurse Saarinen exchange a look, clearly confused by Laura's question.

"Why wouldn't we?" Nurse Saarinen asks.

An image flashes through Laura's mind: black hair framing a pair of wide and innocent eyes. Suddenly, all she wants to do is tuck Sanna into her bed and pat her head until her nightmares stop, until she never has another nightmare again. And if she was Chipped, she wouldn't. But to cut into her brain now, changing her from something that nobody understands—

"Doctor Solomon?"

"I want you to hold off with the rebels. Just for now."

"Laura?"

She raises her hand, focusing on the tone of her voice. She's still the boss. The one in charge. "There's no need to slice up her brain just because we don't understand it."

"But we're slicing it in order to understand it. Laura," Nurse Saarinen says, "you're not thinking clearly. You've been like this for a while now. Unfocused. Delusional."

"I would think very carefully about what you say next."

"I think I should take over," Nurse Saarinen says. "Just for a while. Until you start feeling like your-self again. Maybe Iris can help you with that. She can help you update your fear factors, let you have more . . . "

"My what now?"

Nurse Saarinen leans over. She tries to lower her voice but fails miserably. "You've been talking in your sleep. About falling."

"And how would you know that?"

"I've heard you. When Sanna was screaming in her sleep and I came to wake you up. You know, rechip-ping her will fix that too. I know I can do it this time, and without Lewis's mumbo-jumbo theories. No more nightmares for her. No more fear of heights for you."

Laura lifts her chin. "That is none of your business. When and if we rechip that girl or not."

"*If* we rechip her? See, this is what I mean. The process will work now. We just need this last piece of information. A bit more brain matter, and that's it. And if we have a young test subject to work with . . ."

"She's my daughter! Not a test subject!"

When Laura's legs give out, Iris catches her before she falls back down. "Easy," she says. "Let's get you upstairs."

As they walk away from the lab, Laura waits for Iris to ask her about Sanna. About her having a daughter. Why has she never mentioned it? Does Sanna know herself? Is that why the girl still remains Unchipped? Who's the father?

But Iris doesn't ask a thing.

Feeling drunk, her eyes blurry and aching, Laura wakes up. Something soft and hairy is tucked under her chin. When she tucks her head down, a pair of teddy bear eyes stare back at her.

"You were asleep a really long time, Doctor Solomon."

Laura turns in the direction of Sanna's voice but doesn't get up from her bed. The white sheets feel damp under her body.

"Please, honey . . . "

Please call me Mom.

"Just call me Laura, okay?"

"Okay. You were asleep for a really long time, Laura."

Laura looks around in the dim room, trying to find a clock.

"It's four-thirty. I just finished my last online class for today. It was coding and math. I'm really good at both."

She's been asleep the whole day. Laura sits up on the bed, looks around for her AR-glasses. Sanna walks over to an armchair in the corner of the room. When she fishes Laura's device from under her lab coat, she turns her gaze away from the blinking lights. She covers the glasses with the coat, walks back to the bed, and hands them both over to Laura.

"Here you go. Do you do a lot of multiplication when you work?"

Laura smiles at Sanna, wishing she could give the girl a hug. "I do, dear. I'm just not very good at it." She puts the coat on, the glasses resting on her lap.

"Maybe I could help you? If you hired me?"

"To do what? Multiplication?"

"Mm." The girl nods. "And because you're so bad at it, I think you need to give me a raise too."

Laura grins at her. "Eat something green at dinner, and we'll talk about it."

"Do you need to go back to work?"

"Yes, dear. I'm afraid so."

"You work an awful lot."

"I guess that's true."

"Maybe that's why you slept for so long."

Laura puts on the AR-glasses, turning her head away from Sanna so she won't hurt her Unchipped brain. White envelopes blink in front of her eyes. She opens the first one with a red exclamation point. The message is from Iris.

CALL ME WHEN YOU GET THIS.

Laura swipes to the right, opens another message from Iris.

CALL ME BACK, PLEASE. IT'S NURSE SAARINEN. WE MIGHT HAVE A PROBLEM.

Another swipe to the right.

SHE'S PROCEEDING WITH THE FREQUENCY TESTING. WITHOUT YOUR OKAY. YOU NEED TO COME DOWN.

Before Laura has a chance to swipe again, three white dots appear on her view.

CALL FROM IRIS.

"Iris? What's going on down there? I was just about to—"

"Don't come down here, Doctor Solomon." Iris is out of breath, her footsteps thumping against a floor.

"Why? Are you in the lab? What's going on?"

"It's Nurse Saarinen. She told her crew to go ahead with the operation. When I intervened and told her we don't have your go-ahead, she called the guards and told them to take me away."

"Away? What do you mean? Where are you, Iris?"

"I'm in the basement, trying to find a place to hide."

"Okay, I'm coming down."

"No! No, don't go down there. She . . . " Iris stops to breathe.

"She what? This is ridiculous. I'm in charge here, not her!"

"She told the guards that Margaret hacked your brain and installed a memory augmentation program to take over the city. And somehow, she convinced them to believe her. So the guards will capture you, if you go down there. They'll give you a sedative."

Laura's laughter is more nervous than she'd wish.

"This is outrageous! I'll just talk to them."

"She has a recording of you telling the crew to hold off with the Unchipped."

"So what?"

"So does that sound like something you would normally say? Doctor Solomon, she's going forward with Kaarina, and will continue cutting open each and every Unchipped brain we have in the Chip-Center."

"But she was against the code and figuring out the factor . . . "

"I don't think she wants to figure out anything about the Unchipped. It's just an excuse. A diversion. I think she just wants to eliminate them all. Get it over and done with."

Laura stares at the blue tiles under Iris's feet. Iris stops by a stasis capsule and steps on the base to turn off the blue glow. "I need to get out of here."

"The glass boxes. Markus's box is empty. Go in, change into his spare coveralls, and sit in the corner with a blanket over your head. They'll never know the difference."

Iris's feet light up another tile as she starts fast-walking down the aisle of stasis capsules. "And you?"

Laura doesn't take her glasses off to look at Sanna but she can feel her presence nearby. Would Nurse Saarinen dare to touch her child? Slice her up like an Unchipped salad? She wouldn't. There's no way.

But the lump that crawls up her throat tells her otherwise.

"I need to get Sanna out of here. She's . . . I'm her mother. I should have told you . . . " Laura's voice breaks, and she needs to support herself against the wall.

"I know you are. And it's okay. It's none of my business. How are you going to get her out?"

"That's the million CC question." Laura walks to the door, cracks it open, and listens. No one moves in the penthouse, but it's just a matter of time. "I'll figure it out. Get in Markus's box. I'll call you."

Laura takes off her AR-glasses and closes the door silently. As she turns around, she freezes under Sanna's piercing stare. "You . . . You're my *mother*, Doctor Solomon?"

Shit. Fuck. Not like this.

"How many times do I need to tell you, don't call me that. Just call me mom—I mean—Laura. Ah, shit . . ."

Sanna's mouth pops open in wonder. "Are you my . . . mom?"

Laura walks quickly to Sanna's closet. She pulls out Sanna's blue backpack and tosses in clothes, a lightless CS-key made for an Unchipped brain, and a pair of never-worn sneakers. Nodding at the rabbit carrier in the corner, she says, "Can you carry Mister Bun-Bun under your hoodie?"

Sanna turns to look at her bunny, then to stare at her newfound mother. She nods.

"Good. Here, put this on." She helps put the backpack on Sanna, pulls the girl's hood over her forehead, and nods at the rabbit. "Go get him. We need to leave, now."

Both of them barefoot, Laura and Sanna tiptoe to the penthouse living room, then to the elevators.

Instead of ordering a lift, Laura opens the staircase door and listens. No one there.

"Okay, go. Go, go, go," she whispers to the girl. Sanna tucks her chin against the lump under her hoodie and starts fast-walking down the stairs. One floor down, Laura slides in through the corridor door and pushes Sanna toward the end. Before reaching Nurse Saarinen's apartment entryway, she knocks on a door.

Nothing happens.

She knocks on the door again. "Markus? Markus, it's Doctor Solomon," she says in a low voice.

"And Sanna," Sanna whispers loudly, after cupping her hands against the door.

Footsteps thump inside the room, and the door opens. Markus's questioning eyes flicker between Laura and Sanna. "What's going on?" Markus asks. "It's pretty early for a bedtime story, don't you think?" Markus turns to look at Sanna and smiles. "Not that I mind."

Laura slips through the crack in the doorway and pulls Sanna to her. Then she stares at Markus, pronouncing her words with care. "Listen to me very carefully. In the closet in your bedroom, you'll find a pile of coveralls, shoes, and blue fabric bags. I want you to fill the bag with warm clothes and those vegan bars you like. And put on a pair of coveralls with a hood. Then come back here as soon as you can."

Markus stares at her, calm but muddled. To Laura's surprise, he nods and leaves them by the door. Laura digs out her AR-glasses and turns to Sanna before she puts them on. "Honey, just pull my sleeve once Markus is back, okay?"

"What are you doing? Where are you going?"

"I'll be right here. But I need to do something really important. Okay?"

After Sanna nods at her, Laura puts on the AR-glasses and goes through her folders. Then she starts to type. Her panicked mind mixes words, and she makes a dozen typos. But she gets the short document done and signed. "Send to Dennis Jenkins," she says. The AI's smooth voice replies in two seconds.

"DOCUMENT SENT TO DENNIS JENKINS. CITY OF CALIFORNIA."

A determined tug on her sleeve prompts Laura to take the glasses off. Markus and Sanna stand next to her, holding hands. Sanna reaches over and takes hold of Laura's hand as well.

"We're ready to go. Lead the way, Mom."

Two blue bags sway from side to side, almost invisible in the blue light of early night. No one will be able to find Markus and Sanna, not among the commuting people returning from work. They stop by the holograms and food service machines. Some walk their invisible digital poodles, which Laura is no longer able to see. Too afraid that Nurse Saarinen might track down her AR-glasses, she's left them behind in the Chip-Center.

Still barefoot, sitting on a bench by the Nursery-Center, Laura watches her daughter being taken away from her. Once again. Where they are going, she has no idea. All she asked Markus was whether the man had a safe place to go. He had nodded without hesitation. How he could have any connections left outside the Chip-Center is beyond Laura. But Markus would know more about the Unchipped network outside the cities than Laura ever could. And for her not to know where they are headed is the safest bet they have.

The city looks different in the early night, without fake mountains and ocean views. Laura's too used to selecting her sunsets and sceneries to remember how the city looks without them. The tiles still glow with their blue light, creating a mist-like illusion above the streets. People hurry to their homes. Most of them won't stop to talk to one another or even check the billboards and holograms for the newest products now available in the AR-store. Their blue coveralls make them look like dyed worker ants, moving straight toward to their destinations, hunting for yet another pile of sugar and another quick high.

Then, the streets are empty. They'll come for her soon enough. Lock her in a soft room, pump her full of sedatives and Happiness-Pills. Laura will become a product of her own program. At least until Dennis Jenkins receives her email.

"Sweetie."

The sound is just a whisper in the wind. Laura lies down on the bench, ignoring the cool air that sends shivers across her body. The nightmares have left her pajamas soaking wet.

"Sweetie. Let me help you."

If she stares really hard at one spot in the night sky, Laura can see a star. Two stars. But as soon as she moves her gaze to find more, they both disappear into the light pollution.

"We need to save them, Laura. Like you saved Sanna just now. They're like her, the Unchipped. Innocent. Important."

"Yeah, well. Tell Margaret to hack into Nurse Saarinen's brain and drop her off the balcony, like she tried to drop me the other night."

"We can't access her chip. We've never been able to hack her. She must be stationed in one of the glass rooms, protected by the Faraday cage. And Margaret was never going to drop you, Laura. We just needed you to listen."

Laura laughs. "So you were there. My own mother. What a surprise. Well, I'll admit you two sure got my attention. I'll give you that." For a while, they stay silent. Waiting for the guards to arrive. "They're going to cut open Kaarina's brain," Laura says. "Thought you should know."

Mrs. Salonen doesn't shut down the connection while she talks to someone she's in the same room with—wherever she is located. Too distracted to pay attention to their words, Laura focuses on spotting a third star.

"Margaret will take care of it. But we need your help. Where's your main server located in the Chip-Center? And where is Iris?"

"Why? You're going to make Iris kill off Nurse Saarinen's whole team to save a few Unchipped people? Give me a break, Mother."

"We're not going to kill anyone. But we can access the server and insert malware that will turn off the city but keep those in the capsules safe."

"Ah," Laura says, smiling. "Luna's little switch trick. I remember. Clever."

Mrs. Salonen waits patiently as Laura gathers her thoughts. If they turn off the city, Nurse Saarinen will be left powerless. No computers, no devices, and no stasis capsules. It will also destroy everything Laura's worked for all these years.

"I don't want to turn the city off, Mother. I've worked too hard and too long for this."

"But, sweetie—"

"No. The city stays on. But we'll get your Unchipped out. We just need a distraction. Tell Iris to get ready, she'll remember the Unchipped capsules by heart. She needs at least thirty minutes to get them open."

"They'll need way more than thirty minutes to get out of the city."

"That's why we need a big enough distraction to bring them all out of the Chip-Center."

"What's the distraction?"

"Me."

"You?"

"I want you to shut me off. Take me back to the egg and keep me there."

"Laura, it's not safe. You'd need to be there for hours. We don't know the side-effects that come with long-term—"

"Just do it, Mother." Laura spots the third star in the night sky. "Please."

Mrs. Salonen pauses before she says, *"The upload could kill you."*

"Then tell Margaret to upload my mind permanently."

"Laura, this is very dangerous—"

"I know she can do it. She was already there with the brain emulation program years ago. But to upload a mind was against her morals and ethics, I believe."

"Still is."

"It's my decision, Mother. And mine alone. I'd rather stay in the egg than be Nurse Saarinen's newest prisoner. She'll claim that I've gone insane. Please. Just once, take a risk in your life. See where it gets you. I'm begging you."

Mrs. Salonen doesn't reply.

"Come on, Mother. We're all going to die someday."

"But that's the thing. You won't die, not if Margaret succeeds. You'll live forever."

A cloud moves aside right above Laura. For three seconds, she sees a cluster of stars, brighter than she's seen them before. Their bright light fights to break through the veil of clouds, then they disappear again. She lies there in silence for what seems to be hours. A tiny lifetime. When distant shouts reach her ears, her mother speaks again.

"Okay, sweetie," Mrs. Salonen says. *"Iris has told them your location. Nurse Saarinen and her crew are on their way. Margaret will start the upload now. Are you ready?"*

Laura wraps the white lab coat tighter around her shaking body.

"Ready, Mother." As she takes a deep breath and lets the relief spread through her mind, the clouds push aside, revealing a sky filled with stars. "Take me home."

EPILOGUE
CITY OF CALIFORNIA

Strands of Maria's dark hair fall across her face as she sleeps peacefully on the bed. Dennis fights the urge to reach for the black locks to move them aside. She's beautiful. Strong but fragile. He could just sit here until eternity, watching this creature sleep in her silky white dress. Smooth jazz caressing his ears, Dennis digs himself deeper into the gaming chair's hefty cushions.

Buzz.

He ignores the vibrating AR-glasses and forces himself back into the mood.

Buzz.

The music fades under the message alert. Dennis decides to block the alert and ignore whoever needs him this late at night. It must be two a.m., if not later.

Buzz.

Dennis swipes to the right to see the sender's name. A white envelope icon appears, a smooth AI voice pulling him out of the perfect illusion.

"*NEW DOCUMENT FROM LAURA SOLOMON. CITY OF FINLAND.*"

Well, damn. He's been waiting for this, for Laura to chew his ass out after the failed mission. Not only did he not capture Margaret Lewis, but he also lost a soldier to the enemy. And not just any soldier. Maria.

"Exit simulation," Dennis says. He takes off the AR-glasses and gets up from the gaming chair. Might as well enjoy a late-night whiskey before learning whether he'll officially be fired, or just put to shame in front of the founders. You never know with Solomon. She can be harder to predict than a SIM date's real age.

The liquid fills the glass. Dennis walks past the balcony doors, gazing at the sleeping green city. How he loves this place. Everything it represents, everything it gives. Life is easy here. Good. There's no way he'll give up his power without a fight. Or at least a long and painstakingly thorough negotiation, if that's what it takes.

He walks back to the gaming chair, placed in the middle of the living room. Each room in his luxurious apartment has one; he hardly spends any time outside the AR and SIM rooms. Over the years, real life has become something intimidating. Something to avoid.

Sighing deeply, Dennis takes a sip of whiskey and sits down. He places the glass on the carpet next to the chair.

"Read message."

"HEADLINE: LETTER OF ATTORNEY."

Dennis swipes open the control panel and mutes the AI. This document is not what he expected. He needs to read this with his own eyes. The document fits a single page, something uncharacteristic for Doctor Solomon. It's also full of typos. Another odd thing in a document that Laura would have written. But the stamp is right. The signature. It has all been verified by the facial recognition in Solomon's AR-glasses.

This leter contains an enclosed power of attorney document authorizing Mr. Dennis Jenkins to accesss all SOLOMON FOUNDATION's accounts. Please make certain that he is to encounter no problems accessing the files which he deeems fit and that he is recognized as having this authority. I will be stepping aside from my postion as the head of the Happiness-Program. You may not contact me for any queries whicg you may have.

Sincerely,

Laura Solomon

Head of Happiness-Program and Founder of Solomon Foundation

THE END

Shoot! Book 6 of the Unchipped story is at a close. But don't worry, you can find out what happens next in Book 7 in the Unchipped series, CHIPPED: DENNIS!

My dearest reader,

You are simply amazing! Thank you so much for your support and readership! I can't tell you how much you reading this book means to me. I'm humbled and honored that you've dedicated your valuable time to experience the Unchipped universe with me. I'm still a newbie author, so if you were to leave me a review on the store you purchased this from, or Goodreads it would be a huge help! Short or long, doesn't matter. Reviews are the best way to help other readers find the Unchipped Series.

Want to stay in touch? I would love it if you'd subscribe to my newsletter:

@ www.TayaDeVere.com/HappinessProgram

You can also find me on:

Facebook..........................@TayaDeVereAuthor

Instagram........................@TayaDeVere_Author

Goodreads......................@TayaDeVere

Bookbub..........................@Taya-DeVere

Gratefully yours,
Taya

About the Author

Taya DeVere is a Finnish science fiction writer who loves telling stories about perfectly imperfect people in dystopian and postapocalyptic settings. Her characters are outsiders and rebels who stand up against injustice and form unlikely friendships with other rebels along the way. She is the writer of more than 21 books, and is always developing new stories to delight her readers. Taya's restless feet have taken her all over Finland, the United Kingdom, Spain, and North America. She lived in the United States for seven years but is currently based in Turku, Finland with her partner, Chris.

Best things in life: friends & family, memories made, and mistakes to learn from. Taya also loves licorice ice cream, secondhand clothes and things, bunny sneezes, salmiakki, and sauna.

Dislikes: clowns, the Muppets, Moomin trolls, dolls (especially porcelain dolls), human size mascots, and celery.

Taya's writing is inspired by the works of authors like Margaret Atwood, Peter Heller, Hugh Howey, and Blake Crouch.

Final Thanks

The equestrian world is a funny place. Not like, "haha" funny, but something between "is this even real" and "nothing surprises me anymore" funny. I mean, here we are, likeminded individuals, usually all women, stuffed inside a building that smells of hay and poop. We all take the extra mile to keep our majestic creatures safe and happy. All of us love the sport. Many of us have the same goals, same challenges, and the same solutions.

And we just. Can't. Get. Along.

While I lived in the States, I split my time between marketing, writing, and working at a barn for over seven years. What made me quit the latter? I burned out—three times in the span of two years.

Most of the conflicts that I witnessed or was involved in were purely misunderstandings. People get stigmatized as difficult, rude, crazy, or simply "bad" too easily and way too quickly. I thought about these personalities a lot while writing this book. What makes a "bad guy" bad? What makes a hero a hero? In the end, doesn't it all depend on who is defining the character and why?

But don't get me wrong. My equestrian career wasn't all bad. I once realized that I had met over a hundred equestrians with whom I shared my horsey filled life almost every day of the week. I took care of their horses like they were my own. I listened to their worries, and they listened to mine. I shared good laughs with some. Others became beloved friends and we've stayed in touch until this very day.

And then, there are the few absolute gems with whom I've been lucky enough to cross paths. Thank you, Jennifer, Andrea, Kate, Sybille, Shannon, and Jackie, for your uncanny friendship, support, and love. Now, oceans apart, I still cherish our time together at the barn aisle—covered in shavings and horsey vibes.

9 789527 404188